DARK PLACES OF REST

BRICK MARLIN

Hydra
Publications

ALSO BY BRICK MARLIN

Whiskey Creek Press

Sectors

Blue Lights In A Jar

Land Of The Dead

Nettie And The Shepherd

Seventh Star Press

Shadow Out Of The Sky

Ozarium

Publish America

The Darkened Image

Saturated And Crimson

Double Dragon Publishing

An Ensanguined Path

Anthologies/Magazines:

Dystopian Express

Necrotic Tissue, Issue #2

Necrotic Tissue, Issue #5

Night Terrors

Deep Space Terror

Estronomicon

Morpheus Tales, #XII

The Dark Macabre

Deadman's Tomb

Circuits And Steam

Sand: Strange Tales: Year One

ISBN: 978-1-940466-82-8

Hydra Publications

Goshen, Kentucky, 40026

www.hydrapublications.com

But lo, a stir is in the air!
The wave- there is a movement there!
— The City in the Sea, Edgar Allen Poe

Somewhere, there was a ripple.

SELWYN

Salt water drained from his nose. He coughed. He spat. His lungs swelled, allowing him to breathe again, even if the air inside was thin, very restricted.

But that was the least of his problems.

Needles stabbed his face while something was molesting his entire body. He thrashed, rapping his knuckles against something hard above in the pitch-black darkness. The squealing from the molester stung and he thrashed a second time.

Then a third.

His lungs expanded again, filling with the scent of freshly cut pinewood and flakes of sawdust, forcing another cough. Spastic contraction of his abs forced his forehead and his knees to contact the hard surface.

Tiny needles poked at his lips then side-stepped into his left nostril.

The trapped boy blew out a squirming pellet and

rubbed his violated nose. He rapped his knuckles again, this time scraping flesh, this time causing a self-inflicted sting. Another set of needles tattooed across his forehead, a non-self-inflicted sting.

He snapped his eyelids shut just as the needles traversed.

Then knocked the invader off—actually more than one—earning annoyed squeals.

He reached out, grabbed handfuls of empty space, each side of his person rather than above his face, hoping to find an exit. More needles tattooed his forehead, prickled bare skin on his torso, his arms, and his legs, another molestation of his entire body. The boy twisted violently, flapped his arms, kicked his legs, shunning the unseen invaders. Thrashing became useless, especially in this micro-sized space barely large enough even for him.

Sawdust drained any reprise of clean air, though what he found was when his right knee hit the surface of his prison repeatedly—a few painful hits—he heard a muffled *crack!* As his neurotransmitters exposed more panic, he ignored them, he ignored the knee pain, and struck the weakened area again.

And again.

And, of course, a third time.

Adrenaline-fueled, he planted both palms and shoved, splitting wood, causing moist earth to sift through the crack, finding its way into his mouth, nose, and eyes.

He turned his head and spat, blowing out a chunk

from his left nostril. He tried blinking some of the offensive material out of his eyes but it seemed to allow more inside.

It stung.

He clamped his mouth and eyes shut, held his breath, resuming his attack on the damaged wood.

The crack widened.

He blew out a breath, sucked in a pocket of air—still thin and his lungs ached—as he clawed the earth, slowly burrowing a path out of the blind world. In his ascension, something bitter and squirmy squeezed through his lips.

He spat the squirm out.

His clawing seemed endless. Least the dirt gave as he burrowed further, hoping, wishing for an exit.

Another squirm found the top of his left hand—actually squirms found it, looping around his fingers—and as soon as they appeared, they disappeared. Tickles ran across his face and neck, even a few bites.

It didn't stop him.

He continued.

He prayed for an exit.

His arm rubbed against something hard, the texture familiar, and he placed his hand on it, gave a shove, propelling him upward. Keeping his eyelids shut, still stinging from the grime, he was blind to the moist world against his skin. He didn't even open his mouth, still keeping that shut too.

His arm muscles ached from his dig so did his calves and thighs. They burned and he wondered if this was what athletes felt during or after a race. Surely swimming was easier to maneuver in. And cleaner.

The next move he made, when he lost hope, thinking this would be his resting place, an end to a Wave, switched gears and his fingers clawed empty space. He reached out, dug his fingers into what felt like grass, and pulled himself up and out using his legs, his knees, his feet, and finally exposing his person into a cool air.

Squinting at the bright orb above while wiping his eyes free of the grime, his vision slowed to adjust. And they still stung. He wiped a second, third, and possibly a tenth time before he could actually see, all while wobbling on his feet. His body felt drained. He staggered, caught his balance by grabbing onto something sticking out of the ground. Something cold to the touch. He drew in a deep breath and coughed, expelling more dirt from his throat.

Something scraped the back of his neck, vibrated, squealed, and landed on the ground. The sunlight snatched a wink of chrome before it burrowed itself into the dirt.

What the heck were those things? the boy thought. *Mechanical bugs?* He shuddered. *Geez! Am I ever going to find a way out of this demented place?* He blinked and rubbed more dirt from his face. *Which Wave am I caught in now? Could he be watching me under a microscope or hunched over a crystal ball, maniacally rubbing his hands together, emulating the Wicked Witch of the West from the Oz stories?*

Expecting an answer to his question, he glanced all

around him, seeing no one. Especially who he was thinking of.

Would he ever see his folks again? Mom bustling in the kitchen, making sweet treats on Sundays after fixing lunch once church let out. Dad retreating to the garage to work on his leather, listening to country music. His sister always bugging the crap out of him to play with one of his favorite toys.

The focus of his thoughts swept aside as he snatched a view while standing at the base of a rise. An endless plain smothered with gravestones, the level of the ground making them stick out as crooked as bad teeth.

The boy wished against the occupants of the marked graves to leave their buried homes. It had happened before, elsewhere, in another ripple of the Waves.

Sure, Selwyn, use a telekinetic ability you don't have, he thought to himself.

Single and double digits marked each stone, etched into the stone, as if a child's hand had done the work. The numerals precluded any perceived pattern; no order of alignment. One read sixteen while the next read fifty-seven.

A breeze kissed Selwyn's cheek as he started off.

"Whenever you find yourself in a cemetery, never step on a person's grave – it's powerful bad luck," according to his grandma's admonition. *"Worse than breaking a mirror, causing misery longer than seven years."*

Selwyn's mom had never believed in such "non-sense," waving off Grandma and her crazy superstitions.

Even his dad told him to ignore Grandma's "babbling." Now, considering what had happened and surrounded by this forbidding landscape, he lent more weight to Grandma's words. Treading cautiously above and between the presumed dead husks of creatures (*no telling if natural or artificial*), superstition gripped his spine.

After all, this must be a ripple or surge from one of the Waves, he thought. *Anything is possible, especially here. Everything is on the table, no matter how improbable or bizarre.*

Selwyn climbed a hill, swerving around headstones, careful to not traipse a foot on a plot. A stone archway ended his descent, although a swath of a hundred feet or more showed in every direction multiplied the headstones as he glanced back.

Now what?

Selwyn noted how the stone construction of the archway seemed ancient. Rubbing his hand over the deterioration worn from centuries of weather, though stayed together seamlessly.

The opening of the arch peaked about six feet above his head.

Through the archway his eyes drew to glyphs etched into the interior faces of the stones. Moving steadily, distracted by mysterious writing, he failed to notice a shimmer in the air as he passed the midway point. Nor did he notice the quality of light deteriorating as he progressed.

The hairs on the back of his neck stood up.

His flesh prickled.

But he sure felt the stream of water slide down his back and fill his throat.

A swath of ominously roiling dark clouds hovered above.

He coughed and water fell from his lips.

Gloom replaced sunlight. The atmosphere energized.

Fifty feet away, two ghosts appeared.

Noticing Selwyn's presence, the ghosts' fluid movements turned, their bleach white shapes nearly a blur when they faced him.

They were much too far away to make out the details of their facial features. Selwyn's reoccurring thought of being in the wrong place, wrong time, wrong plane of existence, wrong Wave crashed into him.

He glanced over his shoulder.

The archway had vanished, now replaced by an immense rock cliff face.

Selwyn's adrenaline recharged, ready to flee.

Back to facing the apparitions, a chilled breeze struck him in the face, delivering whispers:

"Who is that? Why is a mortal roaming about the graveyard?"

"No telling... Say, let's steal this child's body and keep it for our very own."

"Can you smell that, my brother? His blood is fresh and pure! His stamina is strong! A vessel of life we shall both possess!"

"Brilliant idea! Two possessions are *always* better

than one. Our masters will be pleased with us! Let's steal his husk of flesh and drain it!"

"Yes, let's!"

Grabbing each other's hands, the ghosts became a nebulous blur, darkening, morphing into a vortex, that swelled hundreds of feet in height. Pulsing, the darkness shaped into hundreds of severed faces of dead children. Their lips pulled back into grins. Their red eyes winked. One head shoved itself forward, the leader of the pack, and directed its collective attention to Selwyn as its brethren followed.

"Oh boy." The boy rocketed off.

Screeching plagued the air in his wake.

He needed to find refuge—anywhere—to elude these monsters.

The huge flock of severed heads crested the hill, now taking a solid form and some bounced off the ground, increasing the momentum of their pursuit. Giggles and guffaws invaded Selwyn's ears as he shot a glance over his shoulder. Malevolently glowing red eyes and eerie voices ululated

Selwyn disregarded his late Grandma's warning and leaped over headstones, leaving shoe prints upon grave after grave.

The heads merged into one improbably huge head, stretched out a snake-slithering forked tongue, flicked the tip at Selwyn's head, knocking him headfirst into a headstone bearing the number seventeen.

Sinister guffaws cut through the air, dropping like acid rain on Selwyn's ears.

Pain wrapped a clamp around his head from the crash into the stone. As he looked up, he witnessed the huge head's eyes explode into its previous state of smaller heads, connecting into thin membrane-fleshed strands. Selwyn saw tiny faces, all screaming inside the transparent strands, some imploding, some turning themselves inside out, splattering gore within the interior of the membrane. Scrambling to his feet he ventured downhill again, lost his balance, tumbled, skidding to a halt in front of a large tomb.

And screamed.

A gargoyle stared down at him. Wings of an angel, clawed feet gripped a stone pedestal mounted above a doorway. The eyes blazed a bright red.

Selwyn grabbed the handle of the wooden door and pulled frantically.

It moved an inch.

The heads shrieked, closing in.

Selwyn gripped the handle with both hands and pulled again.

Screeching ripped an echoed across the land.

Selwyn wrenched the opening wider.

The door opened wide enough for Selwyn to squeeze inside. He barely registered the tingle on his skin and the hairs on the back of his neck rise and the stream of water slipping down his back, but coughed when salt water filled his throat. He pushed the door closed, excluding the creature outside, sealing himself in the silent darkness.

He anticipated a thump or pounding from the excluded pursuers.

But the sounds never came.

Silence shrouded the interior of the tomb and a chill touched his skin.

Selwyn concluded another surge. He *had* felt a tingle. He *had* felt the hairs stand on the back of his neck. He *had* felt the stream of salt water sliding down his back, mixed with sweat.

Sticking his hands in the darkness he touched a cold stone wall, used it as a talisman to move away from the door, pressing his back against it. Yet again Selwyn did not understand which way to traipse. Standing still was not a viable option.

What was that sound?

Selwyn tried to swallow, his throat parched. Goose-flesh scrambled across his body.

Keeping close to the wall he moved, his fingers touching grooves and indentations. Stick figures, animals, and indeterminate geometric shapes in the etchings.

The path took an abrupt ninety-degree turn.

And wall vanished.

And the floor.

Gravity grabbed hold and he flailed, desperately searching for something to grasp as he descended. Accelerating, flipping end over end, air whipped his hair, burned his cheeks. He screamed as he had never screamed before, terrified by the thought of what rushed forward, a sudden stop to pulp his fragile flesh.

Too caught up in fear to notice the familiar hair-raising tingle, the drop of water sliding down his back, a bright white flash, blinding him, sprawling him into a large field, though as if crashed into a soft mattress instead of the hard ground.

Streaks of crimson splashed against a dull, grey sky. Two suns of different diameters and luminosity brightened the depressing vista.

He coughed up salt water.

Twenty feet away, sat an unattended slow-spinning carousel. On the rotating platform were rows of wooden horses, rows of wooden unicorns, one dragon, and wooden adult figures, each impaled between their shoulders, exiting the rectum. Smiles were carved across their faces, instead of pain.

Added to this odd mix were two more adults. They posed on all fours, they were fleshless, bleeding, and their muscles contracted, dotted with a few pulsating cysts.

The heads of the carousel figures swivel in his direction, necks popping and cracking each time as they spun around. The wooden flesh covering the adults cracked and bled black. A gyration dot of a white light appeared in the center of the adults on all fours. The gyration morphed into a visualization appearing on a television when it loses its signal.

Materializing in the air, the shape of a repetitive substance

melted over the bones of a skeleton with its arms wide, its legs wide, formed the letter X. The skeleton's lower palate clicked open, emitted a long drawn out shriek. Flipping on its back the oddity solidified, exposed the bottom of its feet, each pitch black until a tunnel formed inside and multicolored tendrils morphed into a kaleidoscope of different colors.

A voice invaded the air: *Sellllllwyyynnn....*

A servo hum buzzed, trapped bees in a mason jar, vibrating Selwyn's skin.

As the humanoids detached themselves from the carousel, their wooden flesh became human, tearing, suturing back together, as they walked toward Selwyn.

A sanguine path lay in their wake littered with bursting bubbles, giving birth to arachnids scurrying across the ground.

Pop!

A squat fellow materialized. He looked as if he was plucked out of a carnival, the one leading the show. This one wore a plastic mask and tipped back and forth on his heels, taking the chance to tip his tall hat at Selwyn. "Well." He stuck both fists on his waist. "I guess our paths have crossed yet again, my boy."

Selwyn recognized the voice. But, no, it couldn't be...

Guffaws fluttered made the mask shake. "Very good to see you, my boy!"

"Dittle Tek?"

He used a thumb to lift the bottom of his mask. "Of course! Who'd you expect? Your mom? Your *dad*?" He guffawed again. "Hey! Where you going? Don't run off!" The top of Dittle Tek's tall hat flipped open and an automaton arachnid leapt out, sprayed synthetic web around Selwyn's legs and jerked him backward.

His back scraped across the ground.

"I have no idea where you thought you were going, child. There is nowhere to run. No escape. No need to be anywhere except with me. Your world is gone. Kaput!" He brought both gloved hands together and opened and closed them quickly, flicking each finger and thumb, mimicking birds.

"Not to worry, though, the old guy has been decommissioned; retired himself he did. The powers-that-be appointed me as Skipper of the Waves. The Pirate King of the Multi-Colored Positronic Brain Waves. Commander-In-Chief. The Grand Poobah." Dittle Tek sniffed. His uptick of his chin and a quick adjust of his bow tie followed with, "I am here to assist you into your next Wave. A collection of various tales where you, kiddo, will make a cameo appearance."

Selwyn was not excited about it.

"You aren't going to be the star, I hate to admit, only a minor blip."

Selwyn was definitely not excited, nor interested in it.

"So, without further ado, allow me to use this cool toy I stole from some, defunct apocalyptic world. It's called a Hula Hoop Obitor."

Dittle Tek stepped back roughly ten feet and aimed. "Used to be pretty good at this game." With tongue in cheek and furrowing his thick eyebrows and wearing a frown, he threw the Hoop high in the air, looping it around Selwyn.

It hovered at his waist and sparkled a bright purple glow.

"Ha! Still good at that game! Yes, yes! I may need to start playing it again soon, just to get my fix. Anyways. I do need offer my apologies in advance, my boy, your mind is about to become altered...*Multi-Colored Positronic Brain Waves' style*. Not that you haven't ridden any Waves recently, that is. You've been wet before. You've tasted the salt. You've run along the beach." He grinned. "Catch ya on the other side of the pond, kiddo. Or not."

The Hula Hoop spun, shaved away reality and blurred his vision, made him taste salt water.

DECREPITUDE

I can't sleep.

The thing isn't in the closet anymore.

It was. Now it's not.

It used to hide there in the darkness behind my clothes watching. *Waiting*. Waiting for me to get up from bed so it could leap on me and devour my sole existence for being alive. I've lain awake for many nights scared. Terrified. Afraid to rise and face the horror.

...It eats human flesh.

...It feasts on blood.

That's it's nourishment. It's vitamins to satisfy the very blood that courses its veins.

It is the reincarnation of—

No, not that…

Something else…

It waits for me there in the dark either in the corner of the room or under the desk or behind the television.

I've seen its eyes pierce the darkness illuminating blood-red. I also think I've heard its lips smack from hunger.

A hunger ravaging in its gut.

I've begged and begged and begged my parents to let me sleep in their room. I could just lie on the floor with a pillow and blanket, but they won't go for it. They say Ragtime, you're a big boy now, you need to learn to sleep in your own bed.

A big boy wouldn't shudder, would he?

He wouldn't be scared of the dark, would he?

He wouldn't actually hear something moving around on the floor at night, would he?

Someone might call him crazy.

A loon.

At first, I thought it was my imagination; but later, I knew better. When we first moved into this house less than a year ago, things got weird. *Really weird.*

Only in *my* room, though.

I would wake in the morning and find certain things out of place: my chest of drawers would be hanging open; my closet looking as though a tornado had ripped it apart; my television would be upside down on the floor; my window would be wide open while the cold air inhabits my room.

I just *cannot* sleep.

Both of my parents work during the day and sleep through the night, so I know they wouldn't come into my room and do these things. It is the thing I hear, right now, lurking cautiously around in the room in the night's shadow; hunger breaching upon its breath.

I wish that I could fall asleep.

You believe me, *don't* you?

This is my last chance and last request to tell my reader I am in severe danger. And as I write this I think (I know) that it's under my bed. I feel it as it actually moves the mattress, rummaging around underneath.

My parents are fast asleep in the other room because I can hear snores from their warm bodies.

I want to scream, but cannot. No words leave my lips in my horror. I've screamed before and they came running, but I feel like the boy who cried wolf too often only finding himself eaten alive.

Because those were the times when I had nightmares. They were the artificial ones that are only in the deep holes of my mind; growing only when I finally close my eyelids and my body rests.

Should I try again to scream?

I can feel its heartbeat thumping and knocking its hideous sound into my skull. I wish it to stop, but it just continues in a melodic tone vibrating into my spine. My insides register the enclosure of the creature while my organs are infested and diseased with the wretched noise.

God, I need to sleep.

But the need to endure arrives...

I feel my blood chill as a change comes. My hands become icy, turning a shade of gray. My skin crawls and feels as if it dies away from my body. A feeling washes over me as if I am a corpse hidden away for years and years buried deep within the soil in the ground. My skeleton is raw, picked clean of flesh and blood waiting to turn into dust to dust and ashes to ashes and fade away in the tomb forever.

And then, I begin my becoming...

Hot boiling blood injects inside my veins flourishing rapidly into my shell, penetrating my organs. My hands turn into claws. My bodily flesh tightens, stretches, feeling as if it will suddenly rip wide open. My eyes bleed and develop a different color in the iris. My skull shifts its structure grinding bare bone, developing fangs for teeth.

The bed sheets and my clothes are withdrawn away from my structure as I rise to look into the mirror as the reflection of red eyes stare back at me. Blood-red eyes I so longingly hate and despise.

I glare at them as they glare back.

My curse of the dead has now come upon me in its wretched, cold form.

I slip out of bed and walk because I'm not afraid anymore.

Not afraid.

I'm facing my fear, finally.

I've always been.

I am decrepit of my disease.

Tonight will be another sleepless night as I open the window....

AMANDA

The subtle stir of the breeze ruffled Amanda's hair in the bright sun. Her red dress covered her body like a fitted sheet. Her deep blue eyes were motionless, but with possible happiness. Her mind could race back to distant and pleasant memories past.

Amanda loved staying with her grandparents on the weekends during the summer, even scoring a month or two in the fall and winter. They lived so far away from Laconia, such a long drive to the farm, when Amanda finally arrived, she had been bursting with excitement. the first thing she would do was hug Jules, their basset hound always the first one on the scene to greet her, then run inside the house and find Grandma. She'd locate Grandpa next, most of the time outside, tinkering with his tractor or working on something in the barn. Running

through flower-covered fields on her Grandpa's farm

was a must, milking cows — especially Betty, their biggest cow who stunk, but one animal Amanda found very cute — feeding the pigs, feeding the chickens and giggling during the bumpy ride on the tractor with Grandpa became the usual weekend schedule.

If not playing Grandpa's top employee, Amanda spent time playing with Grandma's doll collection. Each doll seemed to portray its own type of personality, according to Amanda. She named one Dolly, one Gertrude (the one with a scrunched in face) one Lisa Lou (her arm always loose in the socket) one Jenny Bee (one eye missing) one Selwyn (the only male doll) and her favorite, Betsy Boo (a talking doll with a quick four-word vocabulary when you pull the string n the doll's spine). Grandpa built the plastic women their own home and it nearly took a quarter of the room. Six rooms, two bathrooms, a huge kitchen, a den and a garage to fit a shared red Corvette inside.

Amanda made this a No Boys Allowed house. Any male dolls were instructed to keep their space away by sitting on their shelf.

Dinners at the farm were amazing. Grandma's magic brought baked chicken and dumplings, baked turkey, meatloaf, beans and cornbread, glazed ham, and not a vegetable Amanda did not like. Except maybe for beets. They were the exception to the rule of finishing all your vegetables. Red, mushy things that had no reason to be stuck on the edge of the plate. Desserts came in many shapes and sizes and delicious varieties: chocolate cake, pumpkin pie (even if it wasn't Thanksgiving), banana pudding, coconut cream pie, warm, and mouth-watering just-out-of-the-oven cookies accompanied with a pitcher of fresh milk on hand every time. When family reunions rolled around, the food tripled in size. If Amanda's cousin Benny showed up, well, the dinner portions would decrease quick, him being a huge eater.

Grandma and Amanda would sit close and knit together on cold nights while watching white, wintery landscapes through the window. Whenever Grandpa shifted in the recliner, fast asleep, they'd giggle at his loud snoring always followed with a smack of his lips. At bedtime, Grandma sung Amanda to sleep, assuring a safe presence on the farm.

Dull moments and happy days were forbidden territory in Grandma and Grandpa's world, something unheard of, until Grandma passed away in her sleep in the Spring. Amanda had no sooner made it to the third, fourth step that morning to wake her by carrying a tray with two eggs and bacon and toast when Grandpa had appeared from Grandma's room, tears in his eyes. He sat Amanda on his knee, tried to explain where Grandma went, a place where there was no pain, no worry of any sort; Heaven, a place of peace.

And it wasn't easy.

Amanda's heart broke. Her world crumbled. She cried for days as Mom held her close. Dad comforted her, wrapping his arms around her, assured her it would be okay, Grandma would always be here, with us, with you.

It was hard to swallow, Grandma's absence, but life shifted forward.

Mom and Dad allowed Amanda to continue her weekend stays a good while after, to be with him through the tough times. Amanda believed they both needed each other. She felt bad for Grandpa. She could always see Grandpa's eyes water when he would chat about something, including the fact Grandma always liked this or that, sometimes speaking as if she were still here.

One day Amanda took initiative and used what expertise she learned from Grandma and begin cooking. A few stumbles at first, a few eggs burnt, four slices of burnt toast almost a waste if not for their basset hound Jules consuming them, she eventually found her groove and began cooking well. Even Grandpa was surprised. Always leaving a smile on his face. He'd even mention some dishes tasted just like Grandma's.

In the evenings if the weather was warm they'd sit on the front porch swing. Crickets could be heard in the woods while bugs lit spots in the air. The breeze snatched Grandpa's pipe smoke and carried it off. He always mentioned Grandma, up in the Heavens, most likely giving God the devil for something or another, just because her brother might be getting away with something, like he used to do when he was mortal.

Amanda had always been a great kid, dreaming of becoming a dancer, marrying a handsome man and having children, even having a room full of dolls. However, all was quiet as the wind blew, ruffling her hair, and her dreams were silenced forever. Lying in the grass her face snapped a frozen expression, not sad, not happy, a solemn one.

Because, a trickle of blood seeped from her temple as the killer walked away.

DIBBUK, INC.

From the same company that brought you alarm clocks in the shape of a six-foot clown wielding chainsaws comes the latest development for waking you in the morning!

Ever have trouble with your old alarm clock?

Has the microprocessor took a cadaver roll?

Ever wake up, realizing you are late for work, finding your clown-shaped alarm clock's circuits has switched into REST mode?

Ever wake up late to find your alarm clock designing balloon animals?

Ever wake up late to find your bot alarm clock has left your room and doing cartwheels outside on the front lawn with the servo yard gnomes?

Well, consumer, it is time for you to purchase another alarm clock, money-back-guaranteed to wake you up!

Listen to these testimonies:

@GriddSurfer9 ☺

"When I bought the new alarm clock bed bugs online I didn't realize it would be delivered in such a small box, expecting a wooden crate to be sitting on the porch. When I opened the package, the servos had been programmed by Dibbuk, Inc. and were ready for use. Immediately, they scurried into my bedroom and tucked themselves into the mattress, cloaking themselves (this I read from the instructions after attempting to locate them for over an hour) using an invisibility processor embedded inside their nano metal shells. The next morning, I was awoken right on time by the bugs as they crawled all over me until my eyes flew open.

@RedBunniesWithAttitudes67 ☺

"LOVE my servo bed bugs! What a rush having them crawl all over you, sometimes tickling you, too! Great job, Dibbuk, Inc.!!"

@InsomniacIAmNot ☺

"Great Job, Dibbuk! There's even an option to transmutate the servos into different shapes, such as a group of Tribbles from the vintage episode of STAR TREK!"

@Selwyn2981

"Servo bed bugs rule! Hoping to try out the spiders next!"

Don't waste another minute! Jack into your console, surf the Gridd, locate our 'site and order your servo bed bugs today!

The first 50 customers will receive a small line of Bodykredd to use at "The Joke's on You, Fella!" online store.

Order yours today!!

*This has been an approved message from Dibbuk, Inc.™

HOLLY

H olly sat at the kitchen table drinking the last drop of her whiskey. She grabbed the fifth and poured another, draining it in one gulp. Then poured more.

Damn that man! How could he do such a thing!

No sooner than the golden substance hit the bottom of the glass, it was swallowed, and left a burning trail down her throat and into the walls of her stomach. Burned, just like the others had.

Richard worked late.

Always worked late.

He was supposed to be home at five; but, oddly, never got home until seven. He was with Her. With *Her* from the time he went to the office until the end of his shift.

Bastard!

Outside a breeze blew, carrying dead leaves that

were as crisp as the skin on a decayed corpse. An open window over the kitchen sink brought in the evening air and the sky held no clouds, as the sun had started its descent westward; the night showed its existence.

In the other room, the TV blared out the news. A boy named Selwyn won the How Many Gobstoppers Can You Stick In Your Mouth At One Time contest.

Holly rose and went to the refrigerator and took out last night's leftovers. She popped a plate full of roast chicken and potatoes into the microwave for three minutes. Then sat back down and poured another drink.

Holly had been married to Richard for 15 years. *15 long years.* The first 7 were great. The romance. The companionship. The sex. All of it felt right—until the ninth year came along and things changed: no more flowers, no more chocolates, no more passionate kisses. Their intimacy became "wham-bam-thank-you-ma'am" as Richard became as distant as the stars in the sky. Unloving. Uncaring.

Holly looked at the wedding picture that sat in front of her.

So long ago...

Both husband and wife in the pic were happy. Smiling, cheesing, holding each other for the camera. Another picture showed them smashing wedding cake in each other's faces. Great times. Great memories.

And now??

The digital clock on the wall over the sink said 6:55pm. Almost time for him to come home.

Late, as usual...

The microwave let out a long beep.

Holly retrieved the food, and sat back down. Steam rose in vapors as she stirred.

The TV spoke of a car crash on I-65. Two people had been killed by colliding with a semi-truck. Authorities have shut down 65 and rerouted traffic...

Holly drained another glass of whiskey and ate.

Least this man can cook.

The clock said six fifty-nine.

Almost time.

Holly finished the rest of her food and put the dish and fork in the sink. She tipped the bottle of whiskey, let a few swallows slither down her throat, and sat it back down. She rose up, grabbed an object off of the table, and walked into the living room.

Headlights hit the front windows.

Richard was home.

The clock said seven o'clock on the dot. The car's engine shut off, the door opened, then closed with a metallic click. The sound of footsteps coming up the sidewalk, soon pausing in front of the door. Another car outside passed by, not moving fast, but with music blaring and the bass turned up so high that the pictures vibrated on the walls.

The front doorknob turned, the latch clicked, and the door swung wide as a tall man in a three-piece business suit, carrying a briefcase, entered. He closed the front door and walked from the foyer into the living room.

The briefcase hit the floor, fell over.

"Hello, Richard," Holly said.

"Jesus! Who the hell are you?"

Taken aback, Holly said, "What did you say? You don't *know* me? You don't even know who your own wife is?"

"Where's Jenny? Where's my...," a glance at the figure on the couch. "Jenny..."

A commercial on the TV: "My bologna has a first name, it's O-S-C-A-R...."

"Who...who...are you? Wh-What have you done?" his voice stuck in his throat, the words came out as a whisper.

"Baby, I'm your Holly. Your dearly beloved."

Before the man could suck in a breath or blink he felt a sting in his abdomen. His white dress shirt became crimson, then a sticky wet towel as Holly honed her craft, sculpting with her blade further. From fingers to elbow her arm saturated in red, she holds her prize, as if finding it at the bottom of a cereal box or in a small box of Cracker Jacks.

Another commercial, a plastic bowl emitting: "*Paarrkaaay!*"

Spots of blood leave a trail on white carpet to the kitchen. Holly washes her under the faucet and admires it with a smile.

Giggling, Holly walks into the backyard, fuzzy from the alcohol. "Richard? Where are you, you *bastard*?"

On the TV, the newsman says: "Breaking news. There is a serial killer among us. Halftracks from Trans

Merrick Corp have been dispatched. Clones are instructed not to leave their domes until further notice."

Leaves flutter and blow under the dark sky.

JACK

J ack throttled the bouncer, taking chase, flanking the opposing bouncer's passenger side not 25 feet from the abstract-shaped building.

The kid's gesture of his middle finger indicated he could give two shits for cutting Jack off in sky traffic.

Jack pointed a digit to the nearest blinking X atop a building's flat surface.

The kid mouthed a few choice words.

Jack's eye dilated. He rammed his bouncer into the kid's craft not once, but twice.

"The hells your problem?" the kid's face materialized inside Jack's bouncer as a hologram.

Jack grinned.

"Are ya nuts, yo?"

Jack rammed the kid's ride again. The face vanished. Another hit caused the kid to white-knuckle the steering wheel, fighting to prevent a crash a burn.

The undercarriage screeched atop a building, crumpling a row of heating/air conditioning units.

No sooner than Jack landed, stepped a foot onto the roof, the kid's face morphed from anger to surprise as the business end of railgun exploded the kid's head, spraying the headrest. Less than 3 seconds after the chrome servo bugs, series 6, drained from the stump, Jack had holstered his gun, blasted off.

When the spherical NARK (Narcisstic Authority Ron Kinnerth Security) arrived, investigated, nearby traffic cams could not identify Jack. Neither could the NARK'S precog scans. Their murderer used a jumbler option, blurring his face and shell. The only information, the faded blue color of the murderer's bouncer.

Three hours later Jack sat behind the wheel of a Runner, a ground vehicle with twin Wankel-McMeyer turbine engines. Flat, dry land shouldered both sides of the road, an outskirt from the colony. The twin suns blazed, preventing the skin on the anti-thermal wrapped passenger in the backseat from roasting. The head jarred with the Runner's rough ride. Inside, the chrome servo bugs, series 5, whirred, aching to escape.

Flashing blues and reds filled Jack's rear-view mirror. Sirens from the NARKS wailed.

Jack accelerated, passing other Runners on this two lane stretch as if they were non-animated automaton yard gnomes for hire.

Horns blared. An invasion of a collage of floating holographic heads transmitted on Jack's dashboard, spatting their frustrations.

Nothing he concerned himself about. His programming gave no "human emotion" software. Turning the steering wheel, the Runner fishtailed, a blur of a smoke screen trailed, leaving the road.

The NARKS followed, a horde of mutant children in Jack's wake.

The Runner's shocks took a beating over the rough terrain. The passenger in the cocoon bounced and flipped and flopped until falling face-forward into the floorboard; a sprawled, ventriloquist's puppet. Three eyed rodents of the land scurried out of the way, making way for Jack's mobile grave.

The Runner fishtailed again, creating another blur, this time masking pursuers with a blinding dirt wall. Steel crashed into steel with a crunch. Wailing sirens diminished; warbled. Red and blues deadened.

Jack rocketed off, arrived at his destination.

The wide gate slid open. Closed after Jack drove through. Electricity sparked along the top of the ten-foot high barbed wire fence enclosing the compound.

The hanger doors were open.

Jack drove inside, slid to a stop, shearing off a tire from its rim, a sliver of human flesh scraped from bone.

Five individuals wearing white military outfits ran

out of the shadows to meet the killer as he stepped from the Runner.

Jack's yellow pupils snowed, a television screen's loss of transmission. Ripples contorted his face into a blank, fleshy sheet. Minus eyes, a nose, a mouth.

A tall man dressed in a military uniform with BROADEN sewed over his right breast pocket appeared. "Take Jack to the Transfer Booth and download his memory chip; delete and replace with security code Alpha, Romeo, Victor, 5, 2, 0, dash, 6."

"Yes, sir." The young soldier started off; hesitated. Glanced back at Broaden. "Sir, if I may speak?"

"You may, soldier."

"Should he be sent back to Ozarium, Sub 1 immediately?"

"Yes. Give him a different face. A place of residence. A desk job. A blend inside the population, better than this latter stint, making too loud of an impression. The young kid wasn't scheduled for decommission yet."

"Yes, sir."

A few of the soldiers led Jack away, out of sight.

One stayed behind.

"Sir? If I may speak?"

"You may, soldier."

"Do you think that this is the best thing for the colonists of Ozarium, Sub 1?"

Broaden furrowed his thick eyebrows. "Explain, soldier."

"It is murder by sending this automaton killer to eliminate Recyclables to keep the population from increasing in size. The colonists have a right to live not die."

Broaden frowned. Sighed. "Soldier, how long have you been with us now?"

"About two months, sir."

"You *are* aware of the rules, no questions asked, do as instructed?"

"Yes, sir. But...I don't know how to feel about something like this. Snatching innocent lives is wrong. Even if they are Recyclables. I had always believed it was supposed to be about freedom and free will in the colony. Heck, those people were lucky enough to be returned to the living after the apocalypse."

Broaden half-grinned. "Soldier, that is not for you to decide. Maximus Slader knows what is best for the colony and the people."

"But, sir, I just—"

"Look, son." Broaden's strict military tone faded. "Why don't you go to the conference room. Take a break. Grab a coffee. This is a job we are paid to do. I intend to do my part. I have a wife and kid to support." Pause. "Don't you intend to play yours, soldier?" He raised an eyebrow.

"Y-Yes, sir. I suppose I should."

"You should. Must I not remind you of the Overcast era?"

"No, sir. I remember. No jobs. No food. Terrible times."

"Correct. Go to the conference room. Take your break."

"Yes, sir. Thank you for your time, sir."

Broaden nodded, watched the young soldier walk away. When he was out of sight he turned, shouted: "Alverez!"

A dark-haired soldier came running. "Yes, sir!"

"Get three others, including yourself, to scrap this Runner and dispose of the corpse in the backseat, as well as any you find in the trunk. I'm sure Jack snatched a few others. Decommission them."

"Yes, sir."

"Oh, and…tell Jakes to unleash the gas the conference room. After that young soldier Selwyn is dead, stick him in a vat for a recycle. Make sure the lab rats fill the body with chrome servo bugs series 8. Give the kid a longer span of life before Jack comes to collect."

"Yes, sir." Alverez strolled away.

Broaden sighed. *Should I feel a sadness for the victims? Recycled, then haunted with being chosen for decommission?*

A chrome servo bug scurried from the Runner.

Answering his own question, Broaden smashed it under his boot.

NEED

Under the glow of a wan moon a dark figure sits atop a building. Sounds of the colony invade its transceiver: laughter, weeping, anger, electric engines tucked under the hoods of ground vehicles, air vehicles blasting overhead in Skydrive.

Tonight, this dark figure has a taste for something different, an unusual Need. Hunger of this item claws the walls of the figure's stomach, possibly enough intensity to power a growth tank, cloning a rose.

The figure licked its lips.

Using its pocket disintegrator-integrator app, quicker than the blink of a human's eye, the figure winked out, materializing in a dark alley, crouched on all fours.

The aroma of Need was close.

The figure smiled.

Inside a climate-controlled Dibbuk suit one of the

homeless snored. The human smacked his lips, grumbled a few words, and, if one listened close enough, could make out the recorded voice of a recorded voice of a woman whispering subliminal messages inside the helmet, stimulating the human brain inside dreamland.

Voices...

The figure became transparent, long enough for a ghostly couple to drift by the end of the alley, walking hand in hand.

Wasting no time, the dark figure sprinted like a cat toward the Need.

Searching around corners, a few vacant buildings, a glass house with a neon cross burning in the darkness, a store promoting the new Selwyn action figurines, a one stop shop medic, and a hotel the figure narrowed its search, noticing a human standing on a street corner. Curls of smoke rose in front of the man's face, shaping into tiny samurai shapes at war with one another.

Crimson eyes gazed intently at the man while the sweet aroma of Need made the figure's transceiver scream.

A small nip, all the figure needed.

Swiftly, the figure wearing pale flesh around its bones, a large splash of jet black hair atop its head, and harbored a palate full of razor sharp points, its body a post-cadaver's transmogrification developed by Vladdick, Inc.*, stood in front of the man who stumbled back.

Hot dogs gyrated over controlled, nuclear heat-driven burners.

"One hot dog please," the dark figure said, its vocal-recognition rattling like bones. "Easy on the syntho-ketchup. Leaves such a nasty after taste, you know."

Love vampires? Wish to be one? Visit www.vladdick-s.com to find out more information.

A LOSS OF TIME

Endorphins sliced through Marvin's body. He bathed in the runner's high of the Zone.

8.2 minutes per mile; split pace 8 minutes, his running app informed through his headphones.

At exactly 6:30 Marvin's hand fell on the doorknob on the front door to his house, twisted it.

"Where the hell have you been?" Tracy scowled, hands on her hips. An invisible cloud of perfume hung in the air.

Marvin tried not to sneeze.

But did anyway, enduring a bad cramp in his leg.

"Running," he said, rubbing his leg. "I told you before I left I'd be back less than 30."

"You've been gone for an hour, Marvin."

"An hour?"

"Now I'm gonna be late for work. I'll get my second written warning, no thanks to you unable to keep enough pressure in your tires."

"It wasn't my fault for the flat the other day. How can I control that?"

"Normal people would pay attention to the low tire light," Tracy shook her head and huffed and grabbed her purse. "Let's go, Marvin. I've no time to argue with you about this."

Who's arguing? "I've only been gone a half an hour, Tracy." However, his watch told otherwise. Even his smartphone. "What the?"

"It's 8:30." Tracy pointed at the cable box. "Maybe your watch is broke."

"I…I don't understand." *Man, my leg is really hurting. Did I twist it?*

"What's *not* to understand? Got a loss of time all of a sudden? Stop looking like you're lost. I don't have time for this. Like I said, I've no time to argue. We need to go. Doesn't help we only have *one* vehicle. I've told you for months that we need two." She rolled her eyes. "See you in the car." Tracy brushed past Marvin, left him choking in the perfume cloud, and the front door shut.

Before he clicked the TV off, a newscaster mentioned a bad accident.

When he twisted the doorknob, he sat behind the wheel of their Mazda.

"Watch where you're going, Marvin! Gonna get us hit!"

Marvin blinked, whipped the steering wheel, avoiding a collision. The driver in the other car sped by, flipped him off.

"Well, are you gonna get us off the shoulder or are we gonna be here all day?"

How'd I get from stepping through my front door to sitting behind the wheel? Did I black out? he thought.

He smelled cigarette smoke. *When did Tracy start smoking?* He pulled onto the road, cutting off a red car. The driver laid on his horn.

"Get me to work in one piece, Marvin!" Tracy blew out blue smoke, snubbed her butt in the overflowing ashtray.

They pulled in front of a tall building. White collar workers were entering though double glass doors. Tracy said bye without a kiss. He wiped a hand over his face, still stunned by these odd blackouts.

The hell is going on? Am I cracking up?

He drove back to his house, limped inside—*man, my leg is cramping*—stuffed his work clothes in a duffle bag. No time to shower. He'd have to change at work.

At work the parking lot was full of vehicles.

The digital clock on the radio read 8:55. Work didn't commence until 10:00.

Usually, Marvin found a close parking spot, near guard shack. Today was a different story. He had to park and walk half a mile. Or better, limp, since his leg cramped more.

After acknowledging the guard who wore a red shirt and jeans instead of clothed in the usual blue outfit, Marvin showed his ID, stepped through the metal detec-tor, walked to building 5. Conveyers ran. Packages moved. The scent of propane from forklifts mixed with the warehouse's musty smell lingered.

He glanced at his watch. 12:00 pm. *How the hell could that be?*

"Marvin!"

His coworker Selwyn stood in front of a pallet jack. He hit the handle release, sunk the pallet of boxes to the concrete floor.

"*Man,* your late! Where've you been?" Selwyn asked. "Jones has been callin' for you on the radio. Askin' any of us if we've seen you. Did you break down or somthin'?"

"No. Not that. I've lost time today somehow." He rubbed his leg. "It's been real weir–"

"What's with the limp? You okay?"

"Think I'll be fine. Not sure what I did."

"And what's with this get-up?" Selwyn chuckled, eyed Marvin's outfit.

"Oh. This jogging suit? I-I haven't had time to change."

"I'll say. No one in here comes to work wearin' stuff like that. Might think you're a weird bird." He guffawed. "We're all supposed to wear the clothes they gave us, you know." Selwyn pointed to his blue work shirt and blue work pants. "Top of the line free stuff, eh?" he guffawed again.

"Uh. Yeah. I know. This morning has been nuts for me."

"Sounds like it. Not my problem, though." He grinned.

"Screw you, Selwyn," Marvin smiled. Selwyn could be an idiot sometimes. "Don't worry, I'll be outta my running gear and into work clothing soon for your viewing pleasure."

"Can't wait." Snort.

"Where's Jones, anyway?"

"Last time I saw him he was in his office. Like he always is. Doesn't want to step out here in the warehouse with us peasants."

"Jones is such a dweeb. Catch you later, dude."

"Be careful, he's not in one of his good moods this morning."

Imagine that. When was he ever? First, he had to deal with Tracy, now it'll be Jones. Well, at least he had a good run. It might be wise to see a doctor about his leg. So much for scheduling another run anytime soon.

Marvin recognized a few other workers, some he didn't. Some stared at his outfit as if he wore a bright pink dress. He did a quick change of his clothes in the restroom. Minutes later he knocked on the door of Jones' office, a pocket tucked neatly into the back of the warehouse.

"Yeah?" the voice had a whole lot of unhappiness in its tone.

"Hey, it's Marvin. I'm here. Can I come in?"

"Marvin? Get the hell in here!"

Marvin heard the squeak of a Jones' chair rolling across the floor. He twisted the doorknob, let the door swing wide, found an empty office.

What the?

"Marvin!" The voice made him jump.

He turned to face Jones. But not the boss he knew.

"The hell are you doing?" Jones' face scowled. The stench of hair spray draped her person. "*Why* are you at my office? You lost?"

"I...um," scrambling for words, "who are you?"

"What?"

"Who are you? You're not Jones."

"First you explain to me why you're late and now you're accusing me of not being the boss here? You on drugs, Marvin? Got a screw loose in your brain? You explained your tardiness two hours ago."

Two hours ago?

"I-I did?"

"Yes. You said you had a flat tire. Now, why are you back here and not on the dock loading that truck?"

"Because I needed to explain wh–"

"Explain what exactly?"

"I...I'm not sure."

"Apparently not. Here's a useful explanation: Get out there and load that truck and maybe, just maybe, I won't send your tardy ass home today. Only thing saving you is we're over our heads. Chuck's over there by himself doing a two-man job. The shipment has to leave in fifteen minutes."

"Fifteen minutes?"

"Yeah. At 1:00."

"1:00!" He glanced at his watch. It bore true.

"Yes, Marvin, 1:00. Not 1:05. Not 1:10. 1:00 on the dot!"

Marvin's brain scrambled to figure out this madness. Jones switched from a man to a woman. Already his day has been a disaster.

"The hell you still standing there for? Get going!"

Marvin started off in a quick pace, in fear of glancing over his shoulder to find another bizarre occurrence plague his day. Such as Jones returned to a male form.

Chuck's work ethic mimicked someone watching paint dry. In fact, he could even do more watching it dry if he was standing. At least he'd need to change positions every so often. King of the slackers in the warehouse, it forced Marvin to work harder while carrying the cramping muscle in his leg. Climbing on and off the forklift became a challenge. Wrapping pallets with a roll of plastic wrap became grueling. But once the trailer was loaded, Marvin had a sit while Chuck latched the door.

"Dude, you gonna be okay? Need me to drive you the hospital?" Chuck asked.

"No, thanks," Marvin replied. "I'll be fine. I'm calling my doctor tomorrow."

"Want a Coke, then? My treat?" Chuck asked. "After loading both trailers, I'm parched."

"The *second* one?"

"Yeah. The same one we just finished."

"Uh...okay." Marvin gave Chuck a quizzical look.

"What?"

"Nothing. Odd day for me, Chuck."

Chuck shrugged. "It happens. You still want something to drink?"

"No. That's fine. I'll get some water out of the fountain."

"Oh, that's right." Snicker. "You don't drink sodas. You're a health nut."

"Yep." Marvin couldn't remember if he had ever told Chuck he was.

"I'll get ya a bottle of water if you want."

"Cool. Thanks."

Chuck walked toward the break area. Minutes later, he came back.

Marvin frowned.

"What?" Chuck said, twisting off a cap of Big Red.

"Where's my water?" Marvin inquired.

"Water?"

"Yeah, you said you'd buy me a bottle of water."

"I never said that."

"Sure, you did. A few minutes ago."

"No, I didn't." Chuck eyed him suspiciously, scratched his chin. "The guys told me you've been acting weird today. You on drugs?"

"No, I'm not on drugs!"

"Yo, just asking, dude." Chuck held up his hands. "Don't get mad at me."

"I'm not. I...I don't know what's going on, man." Marvin rubbed his eyes, his temples, shook his head.

"Well, okay....um, see ya tomorrow, dude," again with suspicion. "I'm headin' for the clock."

"You're going home?"

Chuck snickered. "I'd like to stay and get overtime, but there's nothing else to do. 'Sides, Jones would have our asses."

Marvin looked down at his watch and froze. 6:30pm. He never worked past 6. He took notice how silent the warehouse had become. Only the swish-swish sound of the industrial fans built into the walls overhead could be heard. Everyone had gone.

Chuck opened a door to go outside. Marvin limped after him. "Chuck! Wait up!"

Marvin caught the door before it shut, stepped outside. Stopped. No lights shone in the guard shack. The parking lot had emptied out. And no sign of Chuck.

He couldn't get into the guard shack to open the gate because of the locked door, so he had to climb over. Not a fun endeavor with his leg cramped. He also noticed his car had vanished.

What the hell is going on? Am I having a break-down? Dreaming? How am I gonna pick up Tracy? God, she'll be pissed!

Headlights speared the dark, pulled into the lot, drawing beside Marvin. The air flavored burning oil.

The passenger window rolled down. An older man looked at Marvin. "You Mr. Lanser?"

"Yeah."

The guy's face brightened. "You called a cab a while ago?"

"Um…"

"Wait. Naw. That ain't right. Think it was a woman who called it in. Said," he reached in his shirt pocket and took out a small piece of paper, "she got a ride home."

"A ride home? Tracy?"

"Yep. That's her name."

"Good. Girlfriend or something?"

"Wife."

"Ah, makes sense." He sniffed.

Wish making sense of this entire day were true, man, Marvin thought.

"Still need that ride?"

"Sure." Marvin slipped in back, engulfed in the reek of stale tobacco and some underlying odor he could only hope was not vomit.

"Where to?"

"212 Bank Street."

"The old part or the new?"

"Old or new?"

"Yeah."

Marvin had never heard of a new or an old part of his street. "The old part, I suppose."

"You got it."

They rode in silence until pulling up in front of his house. The porch light threw a glow over the front lawn. An orange glow lit up behind the front window.

"How much do I owe you?" Marvin winced, rubbed his leg.

The cabby told him, Marvin paid, peeled himself out.

"You okay? Need help inside your house?"

"I'll be fine. Thanks."

"No problem. Thanks for using our taxi service, have a safe day, have a great day! Please, call again. The cab vibrated and lifted off the ground, shot into the sky.

Marvin blinked back a shock. *Did that car shoot into the sky?* He hurried into the house.

"Tracy, I'm not sure what happened after this morning. I'm so sorry. I've lost track of time somehow. I…"

A living room with different furniture and walls shaded with light blue with a vintage TV blaring sent Marvin more into the land of confusion.

"Tracy? You here?"

"Mr. Lanser."

Marvin looked behind him.

"Mr. Lanser."

Marvin peeked in the kitchen.

"Down here, sir."

A man in a 3-piece suit sat behind a desk on the screen of an old black and white TV.

"Hello. I'm Harold, Mr. Lanser. How are you today, sir?"

Marvin blinked. "Confused."

"I'm sure you are. And allow me to apologize for me and the staff. Please, have a seat. Rest your leg. There is something we must discuss."

Marvin eased into a recliner.

"First off, again, I must express my deepest apologies and take full responsibility in your entire day. We at R– "

"How can you be speaking to me from my TV?"

"It's the only receiver we can use right now. Calling

your cell or landline would only have our number appear as Unknown. We would be afraid you would not answer. Allow me to express how sorry we are for all of this."

"Explain?"

"Your current situation."

"Oh."

"I must admit to you I failed in my work, there is the right protocol to follow when things like this happens. I let this go on longer than it should have, only because I was scrambling around on this laptop, trying to fix the problem. The problem I have, is I am by far tech savvy. I have the utmost respect for all of my clients, Mr. Lanser. I usually do not make mistakes. But, as you know, we all cannot be perfect. Right?"

Marvin agreed.

"Mr. Lanser, I work at Residual Removal, Inc. We take care of ghosts who get lost inside what is called the Wake, a limbo state, and slip into the Zaphnurr Phase which is a time-slip. Sometimes it's a challenge to locate the person when this happens. Due to paranormal laws, and a lot of red tape, it sometimes takes longer than a single day to fix things. It could take months. Worse cases are up to a year. When this happens, the ghost is not only confused, but finds him or her in a mental institution. From there, we find it very hard to bring the client's mind back to reality. With me so far?"

"I…think so."

"Good. In your case, Mr. Lanser, I located you pretty quick. For you the past 12 hours has only been 30 minutes for me. Crazy, huh? As I said before, my deepest apologies for your horrible day, Mr. Lanser. You should have been removed from your world as soon as the car caused your demise."

Marvin blinked. "Car? What car? Am I dead?"

"Unfortunately so, Mr. Lanser."

"How? How did I die?"

"Right before you turned on your street during your run a car jumped the curb and hit you, running over your leg, then your body. The reason you don't have the recollection of the accident is because that part was erased from your brain seconds after your death. My company does not want our clients to go through life knowing they endured gruesome deaths. Dying of old age or cancer we allow. In most cases their bodies are filled with pain killers before death, comfort meds, not feeling anything.

"But when cases like yours, or even cases involving horrible deaths, we take the initiative to remove the memory."

"So," Marvin's mind whirled, "you work for a company called Residual Removal, Inc.?"

"That is correct."

"And your company locates the dead who get lost in translation?"

"That is also correct. See, what happens is the client slips into a sink hole, this Zaphnurr Phase you fell in. You wouldn't believe how many different sink holes are out there. Some much more bizarre than yours. Consider yourself lucky."

"Huh."

"Now, what we must do, is to make sure you choose the right door. Walk down the hallway and find the door marked with a 6. It'll take you into the Wake and from there you'll be instructed where to go."

Marvin peeked down the hall.

"There's nothing to worry about, Mr. Lanser. You are well on your way to your ghostly life. Again, my deepest apologies for this terrible day. Take care. Hopefully you will not have to see me again.

"Good luck, take care, sir."

The screen switched off. Marvin limped to the door marked 6. After he stepped through, the six dropped upside down.

Harold's voice echoed in the living room. "Damn. Jenny? Hey, I messed up again. Can you send me to a representative in the Wake? Sure, I'll hold."

WOODBURY

The October wind blew through the small town of Woodbury pushing out the remains of summer from its grip, sending it back to its grave until it is born again, shortly, after the stint of spring. The brittle and dead leaves fall from the trees, drift down, glide through the air, carried by the wind. Branches stretch out, hang down, and form into claw-like hands, as if they could reach down and snatch small children up and devour their flesh and blood.

Fields of tall grass sway back and forth, like waves rolling in the ocean. Some fields, chest-high and deep with stalks of corn, hold a demented-looking figure impaled on a wooden cross. Fabric is stretched over its stuffed head like skin, its body is thick with straw for its innards, and ragged clothes that had seen harsh seasons, year after year, have faded in color make up its soft-shell frame.

Black crows sit close by, off to the side, on a tree branch.

Along with the wind comes a large shadow flying through the night sky. It holds no form or shape. Only a writhing black mass that spreads itself out like a bird as it flies, searching.

Below, a house sits on the outskirts of Woodbury...

The Donner's house is not small. It is large enough to hold the family of the two adults and their five children. Mr. Donner had even built the place himself.

Outside, the shutters bang back and forth and slap the wood siding. Inside, both the husband and wife sit close to the fireplace, warming their bones from the orange flames that crackle and lick the air. Mr. Donner sits quietly in one chair and reads from the Bible, while Mrs. Donner sits in another and knits.

Upstairs their children lay fast asleep, pleasant dreams play scene after scene in their heads. The first child dreams of running wild in a toy store, grabbing every toy that he could possibly clasp in his little hands until he holds a tall, leaning tower of toys that sway back and forth; the second child dreams of eating as much candy that she possibly shove into her little mouth from a banquet hall full of sugar-coated treats; the third child dreams of trick or treating, dressing in a ghoulish-looking outfit, and scaring the poop out of other boys and girls; the fourth child dreams of riding on a pony across the western plains; and, finally, the fifth child dreams of being the sheriff of the western town of Blood Creek, a pistol hanging on each hip.

Unfortunately, their parents think that Halloween is the day of the devil, cowboys are violent, ponies are dangerous, candy is bad for a young child's teeth, and toys can be dangerous - according to the manufacturer recalls that seem to occur occasionally. Mr. and Mrs. Donner especially shun the thoughts of masquerading around Woodbury on Halloween in costumes either hideous-looking, or as innocent and pleasant as a fairy.

The laws under the Donner's roof are firm in the beliefs, too. If they are broken, the punishment would be to sit in the dark room behind the little door tucked away in the attic full of dust, dirt, cobwebs and whatever else creeps and crawls in the darkness until the child thinks that his or her sins are cleansed—which, is usually upon the discretion of Mr. or Mrs. Donner.

The large shadow claws its way across the night sky, as if it were opening wounds in the air, and slips in front of the full moon. To the naked eye, it would only be a speck of blackness.

Slowly, like a hawk hunting its prey, it descends downward toward the Donner place.

Before Mr. Donner can turn the next page in his Bible and continue the read about Sodom and Gomorrah, with a blink of an eye the shadow slides through a wall of the house, through the brick and mortar, and slices through each of the small sleeping warm-bodied children like a blade. Ice courses their veins as their bodies begin a sinister process with their small bones shifting, twisting inside of their flesh; their teeth press through bleeding gums and grow, becoming sharp and pointed; and rising like vampires, they slip out of bed and descend downstairs toward their parents with hate coursing their thoughts holding something sharp in their grip...

Mrs. Jenkin's house wasn't far from the Donner's. She did not live alone, either, accompanied with her only daughter and her five cats. The cats – Muffin, Rudy, Sassy, Selwyn, Tommy Boy, and Sally Sue - meow, almost in unison, and are ready to be fed. Their tails curl, straighten, and curl again. Mrs. Jenkins has always fed them the same hour, each, and every night.

As she calls them each by their name—Muffin, Rudy, Sassy, Selwyn, Tommy Boy, and Sally Sue—the shadow swoops down out of the sky and enters through a wall of her house.

Ice courses through her daughter's blood. The cats yowl in a high-pitched voice and the hair on their backs stand straight up.

The hair on the back of Mrs. Jenkin's neck does the same.

"Oh, my!" Mrs. Jenkin exclaims with a shudder down her spine. "What is wrong with my babies?" she asks the cats.

Their only reply is their continuous yowling.

Her daughter, though, who was sound asleep upstairs awakes, while her insides shifts, relocates, and forms. Her eyes open and she slides out of bed and grabs the long scissors from a drawer in her mother's sewing table—the same tool her mother uses to cut her daughter's beautiful blonde hair when she has had too much to drink, thinking of herself a beautician; added to the repeated clippings of skin off her daughter's ears.

Slowly she descends the stairs, step by step...

Edward has not gone to sleep yet. He is late getting to bed because he sits in the bathtub playing with his toy pirate ship under the roof of his house, which, is not far away from Mrs. Jenkin's house, and closer to downtown Woodbury.

Tonight G.I. Joe leaves his mini-submarine and swims to the surface to climb aboard a pirate ship, fight off the pirates, and save New York City.

Before G.I Joe can get close enough to the ship, a huge yellow object, its beak orange and both of its eyes black as coal, emerges out of the water and attacks him.

In the fight, right before The Great American Hero can slay the beast - the rubber ducky - Edward's mom calls for him. "Edward! Time for bed!" his mom yells from down the hallway.

"Aw! Mom! G.I. Joe hasn't saved New York yet!" Edward pleads.

"He can save New York tomorrow. Get to bed! School is tomorrow."

"Damnit!"

"*What* did you say?" Edward can hear her walking toward the door, until her voice is directly behind it. "Did you say what I *think* you said?"

"Uhhh...Nope."

"I hope not! Your father would be very angry if you said that. Now, c'mon! Get to bed."

"*Aw*right!" At her words, he shuddered. He knew his father's anger well.

The sound of her footsteps drifted away, down the hall.

The top of Edward's house is covered in black shingles and the shadow slithers out of the sky and slips through them as if they were thin as cobwebs.

Leaving the attic, it slips through the ceiling, and forms into a shape of a hand. Icy fingers touch the base of Edward's spine and he feels his blood run cold as his bones shifted inside his flesh. Though there is no pain, a malevolence that can only be fed until it satisfies.

Edward rises out of the tub, steps out on the tile, while the water cascades off his body. He reaches for his father's straight razor that lies on the sink.

In the mirror, he focuses on his appearance.

The skin on his face has turned ash-gray, transparent over the ugly bruise made by his father's knuckles earlier that morning, and is stretched taut over the skull. Black splotches slowly color the surface of his skin and his eyes are pitch-black. Dread and hate lies behind them. His lips lift into a smile to reveal his pointy teeth.

"Momma, could you please come here?" he asks, and can hear her footsteps return as he holds the straight razor high, over his head, while it sparkles in the light...

Barry is Woodbury's town drunk. His house sits in the middle of town. He has a car – doesn't drive much anymor'cause The Law took his license away – and it sits in his driveway with four flat tires.

Smoke from his chimney drifts in the air and the wind catches it and blows it away.

In front of the fireplace is a bottle of whiskey, about a swallow left inside, and is tipped over on the floor. The big snoring body of Barry sits in an old dilapidated chair and he hangs his head down, his chin touching his chest.

The shadow slid through the walls of Barry's house and through Barry like a huge pendulum blade.

Poor drunken Barry continues to sleep and snore.

But the child buried under the floorboards of his house rises from the dead, breaks through the wood, crawls out, and grabs the poker in front of the fireplace. Right before Barry's right eyelid raises, and he hears a small footstep, the metal point slides into his socket. And swivels...

As the wind blows the shadow makes its way into downtown Woodbury, forms into a shape of a man out of a fairy tale who plays a musical pipe, and lands on two feet.

Tonight was feeding time for this mass of evil. It needed souls. And now Woodbury, within minutes, has fallen under its

fate like the adults: the late Mr. and Mrs. Donner; the late Mrs. Jenkins; the late drunken/murderer Barry; and the others who perhaps had still been awake, or not, oblivious to the fact of death upon them before it was too late feeling either the tip of a blade, or the stab of a pair of scissors, break through their skin caused by small, fragile hands of a child.

This man who stands in the street lifts his instrument to his lips and plays a tune. The notes drift in the air and lures out not rats, but a long line of children from the darkness now murderers. They each drag an adult corpse by the hand with them, as if they were merely over-sized dolls.

The demonic musician of Woodbury plays a tune and the notes flutter in the air as the long line of children obediently follow him onward, toward the town of Hampshire holding knives, straight razors, cleavers, and hatchets.

All are off to collect more children for harvest, collect more murders of the sinful adults, until the shadow of evil covers the surface of the planet like a blanket and an apocalypse slowly begins...

BODY IN THE CANAL

Mourners stand under a falling rain while the preacher spoke about God and how much He will take care of the deceased who lies in the wooden casket as it is slowly lowered into the Earth. Words from the preacher's mouth assured the loved ones this man, Donald, is not in any pain, he has stepped through the gates into Heaven.

Donald had lived a good life, an innocent life, according to the preacher. He had been even orphaned as a fourteen year-old, and remanded to the state until his eighteenth birthday.

At the state's expense he attended college, graduated with honors, started his own business, and then married. He was a loving husband and a devoted father and an active member of his church, a pillar of the community. Admired, loved.

But, as with us all, it ends like this...

The October wind blows out of the east and the rain

rides along as if it were floating across the sky on a cloud. Tears fall from mourners and drift away, blending in with the rain.

Inside the casket the decease's soul still lived. Donald had not been retrieved to lead him into the light just yet, delivering him up and into the Heavens above. No angel had come down to accompany him home.

Inside of Donald's skin his soul moved from brain to throat, from throat to torso, from torso to legs, from hand to hand, from a cold heart to a non-working artery – trapped, in his frame of flesh.

The day when Donald died, he was with his family at home. They had all gathered around to be with him as he passed over—or was supposed to—into the Afterlife. His wife, his kids, his brother, and his sister were there; all were crying, like they were now, as they stood above him on the surface of the soil.

He wanted to shout out at them and tell them he was still with them, not in animated flesh and blood, but here, and had not yet entered into the Afterlife.

It wasn't fair to him to hear the preacher trying to soften the blow of his death to the mourners. It wasn't fair to hear that because it cut the heart of his soul in two. Donald wanted to be with his family more than anything else in the world. But even if he could, he was in fear of the pain he had just escaped.

A pain he left in his wake.

The cancer had manifested inside of him, growing like ivy on a wooden fence. It slithered inside of his lungs and intestines, blackening them with its color.

Now, he was pain-free.

Now, he felt…nothing.

No worries, except the problem of why he still lay under the ground on Earth. What was keeping his angel from coming down, grabbing him by the hand, accompanying him into Heaven?

Late in the day, night fell over the cemetery with a fog that rolled in. The stars above resembled hundreds of eyes peering down, blinking at the planet. The silver moon tried to show its frozen expression of a scream, but the clouds kept placing a thin barrier in front. The wind blew, stronger than what it had done earlier in the day, fluttering dead leaves across the wet ground, and not only knocking over carefully placed roses for the dead in front of their gravestones, but shredding the wilted, blackened ones.

For five long days Donald moved around inside the embalmed body, every so often looking through the eyelids he had to pry open by poking at a few nerves, observing only darkness. Sometimes he could hear scurrying outside of the coffin; he thought that perhaps bugs were trying to burrow into the wood.

And once they were inside, he knew that they would do the same to his body of flesh, dotting it with holes.

Claustrophobia settled in, an old fear from his days among the living. He remembered the elevators in the tall building where he used to work, long ago. Whenever he would step into them, he would be afraid that the doors would close permanently, and he would be trapped. The fear of the cable snapping and the elevator plunging downward and slamming the concrete below would play over and over in his mind.

God, how he hated closed in spaces.

Perhaps it was because of his mother's disciplinary actions stuffing Donald in the dark closet when he was a child.

On the tenth day, though, something happened. The bottom fell out.

Literally.

Suddenly, there was crack in the wood of the casket and his corpse fell through the ground until he heard a splash. Water filled the nose, moistening the interior sinus tissues.

He made his way back to the eyes, noticing the ceiling of a cavern.

Where am I? His voice was an echo.

His corpse floated along in a canal, small waves making it bob up and down, as it drifted for a short time before a large hand reached out and grabbed it around the neck, pulling it into a boat. When it reached the shore, it was hauled out and placed on the ground.

Donald saw light. Something sharp punctured into his flesh-like prison, splitting open his cadaver, while more and more light flooded inside the skin.

A hand reached inside and grabbed him and held him in a closed fist. Donald was dropped into a glass jar with others, all being souls, Inner Children they are also called, who had never made it to Heaven; all who were the forgotten; the lost; all who white mists with a bright blue color circulating in the center, just like him.

Dark eyes of the captor peeked into the glass. The man's facial features were hawkish and his skin was pale; his hair was slick and black. Under his nose was a thin smile showing off his sharp canine teeth, small and pointed; covering his frame was a long, dark gray trench coat.

The souls circled Donald, some not speaking a word to him, or one another; though some whispered and cried each kept reclusive.

Donald tried and ask why they were all in here, but he received no response.

The jar of souls soon disappeared under the trench coat and the light became darkness. When the light returned, the jar was taken out from underneath the coat and placed on long shelf with many other jars full of souls.

The hawk-like faced man stepped back, slipped off his coat, placed it on a chair, and held his arms out wide. "Welcome, my friends."

Behind him, a fireplace blazed with orange flames licking the air. The man's shadow stretched out before him, crawling across the wooden floor.

"Allow me to introduce myself: I am your Shepherd.

You are my flock. You were lost; but, now you are found."

He smiled, showing his canines.

"You have not crossed over into Heaven because you must be cleansed of your sins. And I, Randy, am in charge of that." He paused. "Now, I'm sure that you are wondering where exactly you are, eh? Well, my little flock, I will tell you. You have entered Purgatory. For the last soul that I retrieved," he said as he looked directly into the jar that contained Donald's soul, "I am truly sorry for your wait. I was late collecting you."

Donald wished he could speak to him. Ask him what sins he had done that were so bad he had to end here.

After the Shepherd said his goodbyes and good-nights to everyone, leaving the room, the remaining sunlight outside finally made its descent in the east – not west – allowing the night to succumb to temptation.

Days and nights came and went. The tall hawkish-faced man continued to come and go, always bringing back more jars filled with white mists with bright blue circulating in the centers.

Donald moved around beneath the glass with the others; none of them spoke to him. But there was still the crying and the whispering he could not make out.

Moving from a flesh-covered prison to one behind the glass was no different, Donald thought. You were trapped, cramped, and could go nowhere. And whenever you were near another soul there was a repulsive force, like when one tried to press together the same polarized ends of two bar magnets.

One day, while the sun hid behind a gray sky, there was a small rumble over the ground of Purgatory. Enough that made Donald's glass prison move on the shelf. It came again, with more strength behind it, and the glass jar fell and broke.

And with another rumble, so did a few more.

Upon impact Donald and the other souls who accompanied him left the glass and, oddly, the mists formed into clothed, warm-blooded children.

"Wh-What's going on here?" a little girl with blond hair and blue eyes asked, looking down at herself.

"I don't know," Donald replied. "This is weird!"

One dark-haired boy, a red-haired boy, and another blonde-haired girl emerged from their mists and joined them.

"We need to find a way out of here!" the dark-haired boy cried. "Heck with standing around!"

There was another rumble as it shook the floor, nearly knocking them off balance, knocking yet another jar off one shelf.

Another little girl with red hair and green eyes rose out of her mist. "What was all that rumbling?"

"Who cares? We need to get outta here! Like, *now!*" the dark-haired boy told her.

Donald followed in their wake as they all shuffled out the door.

He stopped and glanced back at the tiny faces pressed against the glass jars. "What about the others?"

"Maybe we can go get help and rescue them," the blonde-haired girl replied.

"Lookit! We'll get caught if we don't get to movin'!" the anxious boy cried once more. "Especially that one right there, Selwyn. He's tried escaping a bunch of times but keeps screwing up."

Donald agreed.

The children left out of a small wooden house and ran across a huge field under the gray-colored sky feeling the warm breeze caress their skin and land kisses on their bare cheeks. Donald huffed, out of breath, knowing his child-like body didn't quite match his old soul underneath.

The ground continued to rumble occasionally, and they drew closer to the sound. They wanted to go the opposite direction, but the house they had emerged from nestled against a huge mountain.

Only one way in; one way out.

The kids ran until they slipped through a wooded area and found a trail to follow. Most trees appeared as if they were dying with a blackened skin for the bark, hiding their wooden insides. Long branches grew off the trunks and ended in limbs shaped into claws. To Donald, it gave him the feeling they could well reach down and snatch them off the ground. Brittle, brown leaves hung on the stems like a strand of dead flesh not yet cut away.

Before the children left the woods, the rumbling became even louder, shaking the trees. And at the very end of the path, the ones in front of Donald gasped at the view.

A huge hill lay in the backdrop of the view where a bulldozer crawled across a massive stretch of land, using its blade to scoop small bodies and dump them into graves. Digging into the soil the blade would scoop dirt to pour over them.

These had once been the souls of adults.

Like Donald and his clan of escapees.

On the back of the bulldozer was a wrecking ball that would drop and mash the dirt down. That was what caused the rumbling. Repeatedly it pounded the dirt. With an added touch, it would drive across, making it flat.

In the seat, sat the Shepherd.

Suddenly noticing the children with horror washed across their faces, staring at him in shock, he stopped the machine. First, anger rippled across his face; then frustration. He shook his head, slapped his knee.

The Shepherd climbed down, the ends of his trench coat dragged over a freshly buried grave. "Well, I'll be dipped in bloody entrails!" he said, shook his head again, slapped his head, and walked over to his flock.

The children stepped back.

"Do you all know this is what happens sometimes when I have to run this machine, yes?" He placed his hands on both of his hips.

The children didn't respond, each not knowing which way to run or what to do.

"Well," he continued, and placed one finger on his

lips. His dark eyes rolled upwards, "I guess I'll just have to place a barrier so that the jars that you lot were filled will not fall from the shelf, yes?"

Donald wondered if there would be a way to escape or not. He wondered what was beyond that huge hill.

The Shepherd's eyes found the children again. "Now, be as it may, that you have escaped your jars, I suppose that I have no choice in the matter. I'll have to bury each of you. Sorry," he smiled, "it's just the way things go, yes?"

Like a rattlesnake he snatched the necks of two of the kids at once, squeezing until there was a snap.

The others scattered as if they were cockroaches under a bright light.

Donald rocketed past the Shepherd while his claws fell on another child and sped across the flat land, heading for the hill. He didn't dare to twist his head around to snatch a look back, either.

He sprinted across the recently buried and wondered how many bodies lay underneath. How long had this been going on? Do the victims finally go to Heaven, or to some other dark place of rest?

He did not understand and did not want to find out.

The bulldozer started behind him. Donald glanced back only to witness small bodies sprawled out on the ground. His entire clan had perished.

He reached the hill and climbed. Dirt caked under his fingernails and pebbles and small rocks scraped his palms as he ascended as fast as he could go.

Below, he heard the bulldozer grumble and finally

come to a stop. The Shepherd called out: "Come back my little lost soul! There is nothing to see over the hill! There is no escape from here!"

Donald ignored him and climbed.

When he reached the top, he peered out over another stretch of land, but oddly, it was greener; not so desolate. A huge lake lay in the distance and in front of it was a small cabin.

He slid down the hill and continued his trek, running through tall grass that felt like silk on his bare arms. A large oak tree sat to his left; an old tire hung from a rope tied to a long limb.

Donald reached the porch, gasping for breath. A handmade wooden rocker sat on one side; a long bench, also hand carved, sat on the other. The aroma of freshly baked apple pie covered his face like a glove, and a smile grew under his nose. Memories came flourishing back, filling his head with his younger days as a child.

Have I escaped? Have I made it into Heaven to be with my parents who had died so long ago?

Donald walked over to one side and saw a clothesline filled with clothes and one large white sheet that blew in the wind. He looked over his shoulder and saw that behind the hill, its backdrop, held a very blue sky. The wind made the tall grass sway, like waves in the ocean.

Still smiling, he went to the door, heard familiar voices, and knew that he had finally gone home.

He turned the knob, the hinges creaked, and he stepped inside.

Sitting in the chair was his father smoking his pipe and whittling a small wooden figure. He would always carve a piece of nothing into something.

The old man's eye brows raised, he grinned.

From the kitchen, his mother walked into the room, her eyes lit up, and she too grinned. She told Donald dinner was almost ready.

He replied, sure, as if he had been expected, and watched her walk out of the picture.

He went to his father. Love and happiness and a deep sadness meshed together, coiling inside his gut for being reunited with his parents.

Father's hand reached out and gave Donald the finished figurine. Donald took it, looked down at it.

And terror raked down his back.

When his eyes returned to his father he was only a decaying corpse sitting in the chair. The blade driven all the way to the hilt by Donald's hand so long ago stuck out of his throat.

Donald stepped to the side, peeked into the kitchen, where his mother's decaying corpse now lay on the floor with a gaping hole in her head where the thick branch from the big oak tree - which had been broke away by Donald's young hands so long ago – and had been crashed down on her.

A crime, not even his family knew about for so many years. A crime, one Donald had left behind in the previous life and had pushed the memory of it out of his skull.

Until now.

In his hand he gazed at the replica of the Shepherd.

Solid, but with the touch of hate in the figurine's eyes.

Donald stumbled over to the front door, reaching for anything that would snuff away the horror. When he stepped outside a noose dropped down over his head, immediately pulling snug against his skin, raising him off his feet.

The cabin disappeared, now a burnt black spot on the ground, and Donald found himself hanging from the big oak tree that had held the old tire which lay off to the side in the tall grass.

Donald struggled to breath.

Before the dark invaded his vision, the Shepherd stood beneath him with a smile and said: "Tricks of the trade, lad. Did you actually think I was that daft, yes?" He snickered, withdrew a long blade, and cut into Donald's gut.

The wooden figure of the Shepherd fell from Donald's grip, hit the grass with a bounce, and the five tiny Donald figures that, once they slipped out of the open wound, hit the ground, scurrying off as the Donald above took his last breath.

"Mmmph! Just can't win, no?" the Shepherd grumbled and took off after his little prisoners.

THE WOODEN PLANK

The thief followed him to Briar. The guy walked slow, dragging along a blanket-covered wooden plank by long chain and manacle around his wrist.

The thief had no concern for what lay covered. The leather pouch hung from the man's belt became the target, rattling with the guy's every step.

The thief licked his lips. Tonight he would score big. Hearing the old piano cough out notes barely in tune, drifting out of the batwing doors of a tavern enticed him to pay a visit and have a drink, one for the road, right after he took care of business.

The guy moved sluggishly, not a spark of a rush in him. His head stayed low, not contacting ghosts who roamed the streets. None tried acknowledging the stranger in their town, much less the one following close behind. They were simply acting out a residual of their past lives.

The guy dragging the wooden plank entered an alley.

The thief followed.

Between the buildings the stench of something rotten filled the air, covering the thief's face like a leather glove. The thief brandished a long blade.

"Give me the bag and I won't take pride in slicing you up," the thief instructed.

The guy did not respond.

"Hey! I said give me the bag!" The thief caught up to the man.

The man stopped, cocked his head toward the thief. "You mustn't bother me, sir. Please, for your own safety, be on your way."

The thief squeezed the handle of his blade. "Not until I have the bag."

"Sir, I beg of you. This is no concern of yours. Leave an old man to his fate."

"Fate comes in many ways, old man. Tonight, you will have one to savor while bleeding out on this ground if you do not hand over the bag. I know you are carrying gold coin. Hand it over." The thief showed his blade.

"I used to be a thief, like you, who could never settle for enough treasures. It never ends well, young man."

"This isn't about you, old man." He pointed the tip of the blade. "This is about me. My night to gain a bag of gold coins. My night to get enough gold to feed Mary and my son, Selwyn. Now which way shall we go? Down the path of you staying alive or lying face down in the dirt dead?"

The man hung his head, mumbled: "God speak, they never see the truth."

"What did you say?" the thief snapped. "Words about a god will not help you, old man. Hand over your gold so I can be on my way. "

A long sigh came from the traveler. "You must grab it yourself," he surrendered. "It is the way it works. One takes the gold from the victim."

The thief used the blade to cut the bag from the man's belt.

Ha! He was rich!

At the entrance of the alley he opened the bag under a street lamp. Ten gold coins dropped into the thief's palm.

"I'm rich!" the thief said. Time to go to the tavern and drink a brew before returning on the road. Or, maybe stay the night until morning. Tomorrow he could buy new clothes. He could do a lot with this loot, why he could even–

Something slipped around his wrist.

A manacle.

He turned, looked into the eyes of the old man who grinned, missing teeth.

"Thank you," His silhouette turned to dust and scattered.

The manacle squeezed, cut into the thief's skin, and the chain jerked him beside the wooden plank. Under the blanket something moved. A head with glowing eyes slipped from the cover. It mimicked the old man's face; now it stole the thief's. The figure pointed a finger and cackled, chilling the thief. "Now you are the Traveler. Now you are trapped by the witch's curse until someone steals your gold."

Laughter from children came from every direction. They taunted. They teased. They called the thief a coward. A fool.

He tried to wrench free of the manacle. Much to his regret, he could not. Doomed for eternity or until someone comes to rob his treasure which had been mysteriously gathered up, placed back in the bag, and hung from his belt.

Slowly, head hung low, he pulled the wooden plank, passing the ghosts, walking toward the edge of town, hoping for a thief to rob his gold and to carry the burden.

BETH, THE HIGHWAY GIRL

Beth had not gotten used to self-serve gas stations because back home the attendant on duty would pump the gas for her. Beth never got out of the car. Stop and go. Simple as that.

And you didn't *have* to tip the attendant, but Beth always did. One, because the guy would also take the time to clean the windshield and check the oil. Two, because she had always thought that the guy was cute. The blonde haired blue-eyed guy had been there for almost two months and, at that time, Beth had hoped he stayed working there.

At least until she mustered the nerve to ask for his phone number, which to her regret, she never did; as time passed, the guy vanished, off to college.

The guy behind the register could have passed for her Dad. Old. Grey hair and a nose probably broken more than once.

Beth grabbed a Coke out of the cooler, hoping to

wash down the after taste of a greasy burger from a dive selling burgers. The bottled water hadn't made a stride.

"Hello," the old guy at the register didn't make eye contact, scanned her Coke.

"Fine." Beth smiled. "I filled up on pump five."

The guy did not return a smile. Instead, he nodded, hit a couple of keys on the register, and finished his defunct personality employed at Gas N Go informing not only the price, but followed with a question.

Beth frowned. "I'm sorry?"

The guy looked at her. "Pardon?"

"What did you ask?"

"I didn't. Just told you what you needed to pay. Is that a crime?"

What's up with this guy's attitude? "Uh, no."

She walked back to her car, wondering why people need to be so rude. A bright red sports car zipped beside one pump. A tall lady wearing skin tight jeans, face sculpted to perfection, no doubt by a plastic surgeon, an artificial bosom squeezed into a halter top got out and went into the store.

Plastic junkie. Beth shook her head, slid behind the wheel of her Honda, turned the ignition over. She could never understand why someone would want to alter their bodies. Obviously, a big city thing.

She shifted her car into first gear and drove off.

Beth's parents moved to Florida five years ago to get

away from the harsh winters of the north. First, snow-birds. Next, permanent residents. She wished the drive wasn't so far. The closest airport topped a hundred miles away, nestled inside the nearest city from her small country town and boarding a plane to fly south was not included in the plans. Not a fan of leaving the ground, thank you very much.

The sun descended and the moon appeared, a silver circle on dark canvas. Beth needed more food and a place to crash for the night.

The road sign of a cartoon chicken imitating the vintage Keep on Truckin' logo for a place called the Selwyn's Chicken Shack gave interest of eating a chicken sandwich. She took the ramp, pulled into the parking lot, parked.

The young kid at the counter yawned. "May I help you?" with about as much enthusiasm as a rock.

"I'll take a chicken sandwich."

"The Big Clucker or the Little Wing?"

"What's the difference?"

Had the kid received ample training in elementary school to repeat the alphabet with enthusiasm, he failed to bring this spark by explaining the difference of both sandwiches, no doubt informed by a quality Selwyn Chicken Shack trainer.

Beth agreed on The Little Wing combo.

The kid hit a few buttons on the register, spoke into the microphone: "One Little Wing combo." He made eye contact. "Drink?"

"Coke."

"Anything else?"

"No."

"That'll be – *Have you looked in the mirror lately, Beth?* – six-fifty."

Beth blinked. "Pardon?"

"That'll be six-fifty." He yawned.

"I thought I heard you ask me if I looked in the mirror lately."

The kid's face clouded. "No. Just told you the price."

"Oh. I must be hearin' things. I've been on the road for quite a while."

"Oh, okay." The kid took her money, gave back the change.

Beth rented a room for the night at a local hotel. She could have sworn the attendant who checked her in and gave her the key to her room whispered something under her breath when she turned her back.

The woman stood there typing something into her computer.

She looked up, smiled. "Anything else, ma'am?"

"No, I'm good. Thanks."

Outside the window of her room a small town lay. Local eateries and a Gas N Go. On the main road cars cruised by, followed by a tractor and trailer, a freckled, pudgy cartoon face displayed on the side, his right cheek bulging with a wad of tobacco. "RILEY CREEK'S FINEST CHEWING TOBACCO" arched over the guy's face.

Beth turned the temperature down in the room,

cooling down. The place seemed stuffy. She stripped down to only panties, rid herself of her bra, pulled her nightshirt over her head, propped two pillows against the wall, and leaned back on the bed.

She pressed the ON button on the remote to the TV.

News about a serial killer apprehended by police in Indiana brought a chill to Beth. Least the guy had been captured. Had this happened here, versus in Illinois, four hundred miles away, she wouldn't think twice about checking out and finding another hotel. Too many television shows where the killer escapes jail could be blamed for her fear. As well as the documentary about Ted Bundy.

She switched channels, began watching a sci-fi flick about a colony called Ozarium. Before the horror of the show started, she drifted into a slumber.

She bolted upright in bed by a knock on the door. She rubbed her eyes. Yawned.

Another knock on the door. Underneath, a shadow blocked out the long slit of orange light from the hallway.

Beth flicked the bedside lamp on, slipped out bed, pulled her jeans on.

"Hello? Can I help you?" she asked.

Whispering from the other side.

She looked through the peephole.

No one there.

She opened the door. Still, no one there and empty hallway.

Waving it off as someone mistakenly going to the wrong door, she locked hers, switched off the lamp and fell back to sleep.

And didn't think twice about the whispering.

Beth squinted, looked away from the slit of light between the curtains. *Hadn't those been closed last night?* She closed them and showered. While using the mirror to brush her hair and put on a light shade of makeup she stopped. Glanced over her shoulder.

Could have sworn that shower curtain moved.

She looked on the floor for any air vents. Nothing. Then remembered the only airflow into the room stemmed from the AC and heating unit below the window, stuck in the wall.

She stared at it for a few more minutes, then dressed. The place hosted a continental breakfast. She grabbed a coffee and a Danish and when she checked out a different person manned the desk. And like last night, Beth could have sworn she heard the attendant whisper something when her back turned.

A half hour later she rolled down the highway until lunchtime arrived.

Beth needed to stop for gas, too.

At the next exit there were two options, a truck stop and a Chevron station, both directly across from each other. Beth chose the truck stop and pulled into a spot to park. She could eat, then get gas on her way out.

Fried food wafted inside the restaurant. A few truckers occupied stools in front of a long counter, the rest of the dining area vacant save for a couple and a family of five. Beth took a seat at a booth.

"How are ya?"

Beth jumped. She hadn't noticed the waitress come behind her.

"Sorry, honey, didn't mean to scare you."

Beth looked at a thin woman, pale, her hair graying, and wearing way too much eye shadow.

"I-I'm fine."

"Can I get you something to drink?"

"Guess I'll have a Coke."

"Be right back."

The lady's skirt swished as she turned, leaving behind an invisible puff of perfume.

"Our special for today is pork chops for three-ninety-five." The waitress sat Beth's Coke on the table. "And that includes two sides."

Pork chops sounded good – even the low price. Beth chose her two sides on the menu.

"Thanks." The waitress scribbled down the order on a pad. "Shouldn't take, oh – *Have you looked in the mirror lately, Beth?* – about ten minutes."

Beth's expression blanched. *Wait... What was going*

on here? Was she cracking up? Why was she hearing voices? Whispers?

Beth rubbed her eyes, trying to make heads or tails of this.

Five minutes later the waitress returned with Beth's food and let her know if she needed anything else.

Beth replied with "Okay" in a shaky tone with a nod.

The chops were delicious. The veggies as well. Feeling better, she recited her father's "Best hit the dusty trail" to herself.

The waitress came by, asked, "Want any desert?"

Beth thought about it, asked: "What kind?"

"Well –

Have you looked into the mirror lately, Beth? Have you paid attention, Beth? No? Doesn't surprise me, you selfish bitch. All I have done for you and you repay me, how? By leaving me here to die.

(Snort)

Why you *are still there while* I *am here suffering in this hell hole is a mystery. I suffer. You do not. You caused this distress for me, and it will soon be handed to you. Pain well-deserved!*

How someone as pathetic as yourself be so inconsiderate and demeaning, I cannot gather a thought.

(Laughter)

Who do you think controls your emotions, your choices in life, your bodily functions living inside your flesh, Beth? Any idea? Huh? Who do you think allows you to breathe in your world?

The way I see it... what gives you the right to be you, the Beth of the world who lives on 577 Strawberry Court, Deputy, IN, huh? You pathetic bitch!!! I could only reach out and claw your face off I would laugh as your skin and blood drip from my fingers while I

– and cherry pie."

The room whirled, a pain clawed her skull.

"Honey?"

Beth's stomach lurched.

"Honey?"

The pain diminished and Beth opened her eyes.

The waitress' eyes were cut out leaving bleeding, empty pockets. Words pushed and shoved around a mouthful of maggots. "Honey, is something wrong?"

Her scalp, a wet flap, lay askew. "You okay?"

Beth couldn't speak, horrified.

The truckers lining the counter had turned on their stools. Each face, each body a bloody mold, still in formation, shaping into nothing human. The family of five had morphed into oozing blobs and were eating each.

Beth stumbled out of the booth, ran toward the restroom, almost knocking down a skinless creature who stepped out of the men's.

The thing spoke, a warble of an alien language.

Beth shut the door, locked herself in. She splashed water on her face, trying to get a grip on whatever reality she had consumed.

Behind her a toilet flushed.

Beth looked into the mirror.

The stall's door swung open and a crimson ooze crawled beside her, stretching, shaping into her twin, though without a head. It raised a hand, waved.

Beth stepped back.

The figure washed its hands, dried them using paper towels, and turned to Beth.

Beth gasped. She could not move, now her back against the wall. Her mind could not force the reasoning of this oddity.

The figure stepped close to Beth, close enough for Beth to witness the thin layer of flesh over the stump to ripple and bleed.

A cold sting across the throat for Beth left head smacking the tiled floor. The headless creature reached down, placed Beth's in place, and filaments of skin saturated the neck to the stump. When the operation was finished, the strange figure faced the mirror, words were forced through Beth's lips: "All better now." A of stretch of a grin. "Don't worry, Beth, I'm here now. I'm in control. I'll take good care of you. I have always been by your side, unseen by the naked eye."

Beth's eyes blinked.

"Any idea what's going on here, Beth? Betcha can't guess."

Beth couldn't respond.

"I'll tell you, since you are indisposed, in a way." Giggle. "Now that you have finally come to reason and seen yourself in the mirror, Beth, *what* do you see?"

Beth did not respond. She saw a monster.

"Well, I'll explain. You are me and I am you, dear,"

explained in a tone and adult would use speaking to a child. "One of us will leave this bathroom – I'm sure you can guess who." The headless body which used to harbor Beth's head slowly deflated, outlining the skeleton. "We have been searching for hosts to infect here on Earth. For many years we have watched the human race closely, studying your every move by sending scouts, especially drones. Choosing the right hosts takes patience. Takes time.

"My race comes from a different dimension where we are at war. Using human bodies, controlling them as I am controlling you, my dear, eliminates casualties. We are realizing the more human flesh we use as troops, quicker we can leave one body, infect the next to use another to fight. You are one of a hundred so far. Just wait, once our mission is complete you will be fighting alongside thousands of your race. So, you won't be alone, unless of course your head explodes." Giggle. "This little parody I developed was all in fun. Horrifying, huh? I could have just slipped under your scalp and snuffed you away. But, I'm creative. I wanted to push the boundaries.

"So, without further ado, let's take a trip into my dimension, shall we?"

A portal formed, engulfing the strange figure and her victim.

A LITTLE HEART

Momma told me Grandpa was in the casket, but I tug on momma's jacket and point at Grandpa sitting in a chair, winking his eye.

'Isabella,' mamma says, 'your Grandpa isn't with us anymore. God took him.'

'But, momma, he's sitting over there," I say.

Momma doesn't even look. 'No, he's not.'

'Yes, he is! Look!'

'Isabella! Don't start! I'm damn tired of your shenanigans, young lady."

'I'm not making it up, momma. I see Grandpa.'

'Isabel-'

'Grandpa is over there and he's winking at me and waving and–'

'ISABELLA! Don't argue with me, young lady. Do not—ever—cut your mother off when she's speaking to you. Understand?'

'But Grand—'

'Shut it. You'll learn to be respectful, child." She leans down, hisses like that old mean witch I saw on TV: "Even if I have to beat it out of you. Want that?"

I shake my head.

'Show some respect, child. I sure as hell didn't give you that backtalk. I blame your stupid father. Freaking deadbeat who can't keep a job to pay *me* to support *you*.'

'I'm sorry, momma.'

'You should be. Do me a favor and leave my sight before I slap you in front of everyone. Go sit down."

I do as I'm told and sit next to Grandpa. He smiles. His lips don't move but I hear his voice in my head. He tells me how proud he is to be my grandpa. And nothing is more special in this whole wide world than me.

"Thanks, Grandpa."

"Who are you talking to, Isabella?"

"Hi, Uncle Selwyn."

Uncle Selwyn sits next to me. Not only does always bring me a bag of candy from where he works, at the local pharmacy, he always smells good. Momma always says it is his aftershave. "Who are you talking to?" he asks again.

"Grandpa." I turn to show Uncle Selwyn, but Grandpa vanished.

"You're talking to Grandpa?" He looks where Grandpa sat. Uncle Selwyn stares and looks like he just ate a Sour Patch candy because his face is all scrunched up.

"I was."

"Huh, well, I don't see him." Uncle Selwyn must have had too many candies cause his doesn't change.

"He was there, Uncle Selwyn. I swear it!"

"I believe you, Isabella." He pats my head. "Hey, look what Willy Wonka gave me today."

I open the brown paper bag and it is stuffed with Tootsie Rolls, Rollo Chewy Caramel in Milk Chocolate, mini Twix Bars, mini Snickers bars, mini Almond Joys (ugh, coconut taste weird), mini Milky Ways, Hershey Kisses, Reese Cups, mini Mounds (another weird one), Blow Pops, and those little colorful chocolate candies in a plastic sleeve.

'*Ooof!* You're getting awful strong!'

'Sorry, Uncle Selwyn.'

'It's okay.' He grins. 'I dig those big hugs.'

'Isabella! Give me that!'

The bag is ripped out of my hand.

'But Uncle Selwyn gave it to me, momma.'

Mom glared at Uncle Selwyn. 'Why do you insist on giving her candy, George?' She pitches the bag in Uncle Selwyn's lap.

'Because she's a kid. Kids love candy, Jen.'

'Not this one. Isabella knows better than to accept all that sugar. It's bad for her teeth.'

Uncle Selwyn's face does that scrunchy thing again. Those Sour Warheads are deadly! 'I've always brought her candy. What gives?'

"I'm changing the rules. Starting right now. No

more candy for my daughter. She doesn't need her teeth to rot out of her skull before she's ten.'

'Lighten up, Jen. Give Isabella some fun in her life. You know, you are always hard on this child ever since Matt left.'

'Oh, now it's my fault my husband ran off with another woman?'

'I didn't say that.'

'You implied it, Selwyn.'

'Implied it? Are you serious? Look.... we don't need to argue about this, especially now with Dad over there."

'Exactly. We don't. That's why I'm ending this conversation. I'm gonna say this one time, and one time only: You bring another bag of candy to my daughter and I'll keep her from seeing you and Beth." Momma glances at me. "No more weekend stays at your house making pizza, drinking sodas, watching movies, or whatever stupidity you guys do.'

'Jen...'

'Got it?'

Uncle Selwyn waits a few seconds, his eyebrows scrunched, before he replies. 'Sure. Whatever you say, Jen.'

'Sorry, sweetie,' Uncle Selwyn says.

'That's okay.' When I try to smile momma jerks me on my feet. 'Ow!'

'Geez! Don't hurt her, Jen, just because I made you mad!'

'Mind your own business, Selwyn!'

Mommy drags me away from Uncle Selwyn and he not only looks shocked, but sad.

'Sit right there,' momma says. 'got it?'

I obey.

'Do not move from this spot, hear?'

'Yeah.'

Mommy stomps off and I'm all alone again. But not for long. Grandpa sits down and puts his arm around me and grins. *Try not to pay attention the way your momma acts, Isabella. She doesn't know any better. I believe things will change soon.*

I see my Uncle Frank and Aunt Mary and their kids. All are older than me except Patty. She sees me. Sticks out her tongue.

Not a Patty fan. At all. She's a brat. 'Specially to me. Momma never believes it when I tell her how mean Patty is. Just like when I told momma about Grandpa being here. Goes in one ear, out the other. Grandpa used to say that all the time.

'How's my little flower?' Grandma sits next to me. She always calls me her little flower because I keep blossoming, growing up to be big girl. 'I'm fine,' I say.

'Good.' She pats me on my knee. 'You look very pretty today, honey, with your white and blue dress on and the flower in your hair.'

'Thank you. You look really pretty too, Grandma '

'Thanks, honey.'

'You smell good too.' Grandma likes to wear good-smelling perfume.

She chuckles. 'Thanks. Where'd your mom go?'

'I don't know. She told me to sit right here.'

'Oh. Wait. There she is. I'll be back, Isabella.' She pats my knee.

'Okay.'

When Grandma approaches momma is on her cellphone. Momma is impatient. Grandma tries talking to her, but she scowls, leaves the room.

Grandma reacts by frowning and comes back, sitting down next to me again.

'Why are you crying, Grandma?' I ask.

'Oh, I...have something in my eye.' She dabs her eyes with a Kleenex.

'Both eyes?'

'Yes, honey.'

Minutes roll by, Grandma tells me about the pies she'll be cooking tomorrow. My stomach grumbles.

'Hey, Isabella.'

I look up to see momma's boyfriend, Bob. He sits next to me.

'Hey, Bob.'

'How are you?' he asks.

'Fine.'

"Hello, Mrs. Hill."

Grandma smiles, acknowledges Bob. Asks how he is and if he's been staying busy at work. He has.

'Ready to go back to the circus when it comes to town?' Bob asks.

'Yep!' Momma and Bob took me to the circus last week. I had so much fun!

"Has the tooth fairy come to see you?'

'Um, no, why?

'Looks like you lost another tooth.'

'Not yet.'

Grandma grins.

'I did.' Bob smiles, shows me the empty slot.

'Did the tooth the fairy come see you?'

'I stopped getting money from the tooth fairy a long time ago.'

Grandma chuckles.

'Really?'

'Grownups aren't supposed to get money for losing a tooth. It'd bankrupt the Tool Fairy's account. Right, Mrs. Hill?' Grandma nods. 'All that money goes to kids.'

'If you don't get money, you must be rich by now.'

'No.' Bob chuckles. 'I'm not rich, honey.'

'Oh.'

Momma returns and sits next to Bob.

'Hey, babe,' Bob says.

'Hey," Momma replies.

Bob puts his arm around her, gives her a hug.

I wonder if I should say something to Bob about Grandpa. Would he believe me?

'Be right back,' momma says to Bob. She kisses him before she goes off to speak to someone standing at the casket.

'Bob.'

'Yes, Isabella?'

'I've been trying to tell Mommy something.'

'What's that?'

'If I say it, do you think you'll believe me?'

'Sure. I'd believe anything. What's up, kiddo.'

I suck in a deep breath. 'Grandpa is over there.'

'Where?'

'In that chair. He's looking at everyone with a smile. Oh, he sees me staring. He's waving at us.'

Bob wears the same face as Uncle Selwyn. Maybe both have been sharing a bag of Sour Warheads. 'Um…'

'You see him too, right?'

'Uh…sure,' he bites his lip, 'he's over there waving at us.'

I frown. 'How do you like his new blue shirt?'

'Its…nice-looking.'

'Really? You like it?'

'Sure, I do.'

'Isabella.'

Momma has returned.

'I told you to stop that crap. Why don't you ever behave, child?'

'Jen, aren't you being a little too harsh on her. She's only coping with this….,' he bites his lip again, 'stuff the best she can. She's only a kid.'

'Don't speak to me as if I'm an idiot. I'm well aware of Isabella' age. Telling me how I should and shouldn't speak to my child is my concern. No one else's. Sure as hell isn't anyone's business.'

'I understand where you're coming from, babe. I'd

never tell you how to speak or raise Isabella. And as far as being an idiot...... Far from it,' Bob defends. 'you're an intelligent woman.' He smiles.

Doesn't get a return one from momma. Only a glare. 'Come outside with me for a moment, Bob.'

'Sure thing, babe.' Bob gives me a quick smile as he walks out the room with momma, passing Grandpa who is wearing his favorite white shirt. He mouths the words 'Love you, pumpkin.'

It cheers me up. I wonder why momma keeps scolding me and wonder why no one else can see Grandpa. Before I can get up and go to him, Grandma hugs me close, tells me everything will be okay, apologizes for momma's attitude. Says she'll act better soon.

After Pastor Tom from our church speaks good things about Grandpa, telling everyone Jesus has a man walking beside him who has been a great father and husband and to watch out, he's a kidder. This brings a few smiles from the audience. We bow our heads in prayer.

I open one eye to peek at Grandpa who stands next to Tom with a big smile.

Momma escorts me outside and into her car. Bob rides up front and I sit in the back with Grandma. She squeezes my hand, leans over, whispers how much she loves me and how proud she is of me before the car moves. Even mentions how proud Grandpa is, too. I look around for Grandpa and see him standing in the doorway, waving at me.

Pastor Tom talks about Grandpa at the cemetery while we sit in front of a casket. We bow our heads and pray again. We all get in line and walk up to the coffin. Everyone is placing a rose on it top. Momma gives me one and I do the same helped by Bob lifting me up.

We watch the ground swallow the coffin.

Grandpa leans against a tree, smoking his pipe. I ask Momma if he is coming with us or not.

Momma's nostrils flare. 'Isabella! Do I have to repeat myself ten times today? Look,' she points her finger, 'Grandpa is dead. Gone. His body is in the coffin. His soul is in heaven. I'm not sure why you cannot believe that. You are old enough to understand it.'

'Jen, be easy on her.'

'Shut-up, Bob!'

'Whoa! Hey! Don't get mad at me, too, you know. Isabella is coping with this the best she can.'

'Oh. And what about me, Bob? How the hell do you think I'm coping with it? I have to deal with the financial part of Dad's death because he received a tiny social security check to go along with the tiny one Mom receives. The man left mom in a financial disaster. Hospital bills. Credit card debt. I have to figure it all out cause my mom can't budget her way out of a paper bag.

'Let's not worry about Jen. She's always been strong. Made it through a bad divorce and raised a mouth to feed on minimum wage. So, let's all hold hands and boo-hoo about Isabella. boo-hoo, she doesn't understand the death of her Grandpa. Boo-hoo, let's give her a bag of candy. Boo-hoo, let's not scold her when she keeps making it up that Dad is still alive and sitting back at the funeral home, as if he'd never left this miserable piece of shit world.

'Sometimes, I wondered why I chose to give birth to Isabella.'

'Jen…You don't mean that.'

'Jen!' Grandma says.

'Shut up, Mom! I don't have any patience left to deal with your crap right now.'

'And, Bob? What do *you* know, Bob? You are not her father. Your only spot in my life and my daughter's is too keep us happy. Lately, I'm not so sure you've been up for the task.'

'You used to take Isabella for ice cream, just you two, so I could get some peace. You used to help me with the monthly bills. not anymore.'

'Jen, I've tried helping you by giving extra off my weekly paychecks. If we lived together we'd save a money and be able to pay our bills just fine.'

'Live with you? Ha! Not happening. You don't keep a job more than six months.'

'That's not my fault. Whenever my contract is up I return to the temp services, hoping for another spot some-'

'Spare me the bull, Bob.'

'You're…. unbelievable, Jen.'

'Tell you what's believable here. Stay out of my life, 'kay? Stay the hell away!'

Bob looks like he's been sucker punched and walks off, shaking his head.

Mommy looks down at me.

'C'mon. Let's get home! If you so much as whisper anything about Grandpa again I'm going to knock the crap out of you! Got it, young lady?'

'Yes.'

Mommy drags me past where Grandpa is supposed to be buried. I look around, trying to see if he's close by. But he is not. She stops walking and I almost bump into her. She glances over her shoulder and I thought for sure she will yell at me again.

She doesn't.

'What's wrong, Mommy?'

She says nothing, let's go of my hand, bends down by the tree.

'What's wrong, Momma?' I ask.

Mommy stands here, tears flowing down both cheeks. She looks to the left and to the right and behind her.

'Momma, what's wrong?' I ask again.

Momma turns to me. 'Isabella, this…this is your Grandpa's pipe.'

'I know. I saw him smoking it.'

Momma scrunches her face. Her bottom lip quivers. The tears come again. She plops her fanny down and runs her thumb over the symbol engraved on the fat part of the pipe.

A little heart.

Momma told me a long time ago she drew it on

there when she was a little girl. She drew hearts on Grandpa's stuff because she loved him.

Grandpa is standing by the grave, smiling, and gives me a wink before he disappears.

ONE FINE MORNING

Sherman's alarm crawled. He flicked the last servo bed bug off and planted his feet on the floor, ran fingers through his hair, stretched, and headed into the bathroom to relieve himself.

Outside a lawn mower started up.

Sherman dressed, told the voice-activated Jolt Maker to make him a cup of coffee and peeked through the window: blue skies and a bright sun reflected a pleasant day. Sherman sipped his coffee and watched a squirrel scurry atop the wooden privacy fence, take a leap into a tree that shaded Chris's swing set.

Sherman forced back sadness before it could manifest, still recollecting the car crash. The tires sliding on wet pavement. The faulty seatbelt ripping in half. Chris' small body shooting out the back passenger window, the pavement catching the fall.

A newscaster on the living room wall screen spoke about the continuing cyber war, the high price of oil, riots across the States, while a group of employees from the Bank & Trust congealed together, smiled—even though stocks were plummeting—and rang the NYSE bell. The newsman reminded all colonists are instructed to use the roads today. Air travel is prohibited. Another sniper has been shooting hover cars out of the sky. Agents are searching for the criminal.

Before stepping through the door in the bay, Sherman failed to notice the long-faced man following his every move through each room's wall vid in the vault.

The ceiling slid open. Sherman used the turbines to lift, then set his quad on the street. Fresh cut grass wafted inside as he rolled down his window.

Carl still wished to use a push mower, brought up before the world changed. He worked hard, too, always keeping the lawn nice. Sherman wondered if he would have the chance to do the same once his employer Trans-Merrick allowed him to retire.

Sherman waved at Carl. The old man shielded sunlight from his eyes, squinted, but didn't return the gesture. The mower sputtered to silence as he let go of the handle. Carl stared, blank-faced.

Sherman said, 'Hey, Carl, how are you this fine morning?'

Carl blinked.

"Something wrong, buddy?"

Another blink, even a frown.

Sherman glanced over his shoulder. Nope, nothing but more lawns and an empty street.

Sherman tried acknowledging Carl again, once again a failure, then shifted the vehicle in gear. In his rearview mirror, Sherman caught Carl watching him leave. Sherman worried about him. It was never rare Carl to act odd. The guy was a pleasant person. Always friendly. Always inviting Sherman over for a beer.

Sherman switched channels on the radio until locating the selected channel Trans-Merrick approved for the day. All other channels were mute. Sherman couldn't wait for Friday when he could listen to the blues music channel, not this techno elevator rap tune.

A few quads whizzed past once he turned onto a junction, looping him around to his exit. At the stoplight he had an odd feeling he was being watched. A small face gazed out of a passenger window without emotion.

Sherman smiled, but the little girl did not return it back.

What the hell is up with people this morning? he thought.

When the light turned green the little face pressed against the glass, attempting to gain a better look. Sherman let off the accelerator, allowed the other quad to move ahead.

Sherman never enjoyed people staring at him. Today birthed an unsettling.

Quads passing him. More small faces pressed against the glass, staring. Even a few drivers craned their necks to look at him.

Sherman figured it'd be wise for them to keep their eyes on the road, and not on him. His brain couldn't muster an explanation for all the stares. Was something wrong with my quad? Had somebody vandalized the paint during the night? No, couldn't be. The alarm system would have screamed.

Curious, he checked for vandalism anyway and pulled into a charging station. He took a stroll around the vehicle. No marks of any kind.

Strange.

Sliding behind the wheel he noticed the people who had plugged in, charging their own quad, staring at him. An old-timer, still using gas in his vintage quad, over-filled the tank while fuel poured out.

The guy didn't seem to notice.

Sherman wondered if everyone in town had gone nuts. Had he taken 3 blue pills too many to help him sleep?

He drove onto the highway and a semi-truck failed to switch lanes so he could merge. Pavement ran its course and Sherman cruised along the shoulder, kicking gravel. Riley Creek's Finest Chewing Tobacco displayed on the trailer with the swell of an animated cartoon face: big blue eyes, freckles, a straw hat resting on its head, and one cheek stuffed with a chew.

The holo character winked.

Then turned to the side and spit.

Sherman slowed, got behind the truck. He intended on passing this insensitive idiot and flipping him off. He punched it, sped around the truck, tried to see the driver, but couldn't. The driver's window was tinted.

At least he didn't notice that driver's face staring at him.

Sherman arrived at his job and took the elevator to the 10th floor. Rows of cubicles ran north, south, east, and west. Employees were jacked into their consoles, working in the virtual world.

A few heads lifted. Eyes followed Sherman.

Sherman noticed one who wasn't logged in. "Sam," he said, "you're not gonna believe my morning, man. Things are weirded out. People keep giving me blank stares."

Sam didn't turn around.

"Earth to Sam. Exit your window, dude. Listen to this stuff."

Sam faced forward.

"Um. Sam. Hey, man. Can't you hear me?" Sherman touched the tall man's shoulder.

Sam turned.

First, Sherman noticed Sam's blank face. Second, he listened as Sam spoke in a monotone voice: "Systematic failure dash 632."

Sam stood, his headphones pulled from his head.

"What's wrong with you?" Sherman asked.

Other employees stood. A litter of flesh and blood and blank stares.

"Systematic failure dash 632," they chanted.

"Systematic, what?" Sherman said.

"Systematic failure dash 632. Do not move. Any more movements will impair neurotransmitter reboot."

Sherman backed away.

"Movements will impair reboot."

Sherman sprinted to the elevator.

"Initializing next sequence."

Employees moved toward Sherman.

The digital above read 5th floor and the red arrow pointed down. Pressing the button repeatedly did nothing to speed the process.

Employees moved toward him.

The doors opened, Sherman slipped inside. As they closed, Sherman saw Sam in the lead reaching out a hand for him.

When they reopened he made for an escape only to grabbed by 2 employees and dragged backward. He fought to break their hold. Both mouths informed him: "Neurotransmitter reboot initiated in 3...2...1..."

—darkness.

Sherman awoke soaking in a vat. Multiple tubes connected to parts of his flesh. A robot gazed at him through the glass.

"Sherman 7, you have exceeded your presence in the program. Failure to follow the rules has cost you a pass to act as a human again. Posing as a human male beyond time allowed inside the program has cost you, under the bylaws written by Trans-Merrick, section 69873. You will be cloned as a solid object and returned to the program indefinitely. Please reread your initial instructions for all pre-existing organisms."

After the fall of humanity Earth's apocalyptic world became a graveyard of bones until the birth of Trans Merrick, a corporation producing virtual worlds for spores birthed inside vats. You can choose which organism you would like to be.

"Multiple choices include a tree, a leaf, a branch, a flower, a bush, a blade of grass, a rock, a small patch of pavement. Anything else you can think of could be allowed except imitating a mortal.

"Please make your choice, Sherman. Trans-Merrick is very happy for your return."

SPRAY ON SELLY

From the same company that brought you servo bed bugs comes Spray on Selly, a synthetic tearaway spray applied on one's clothing when one wishes to visit a smoke-filled environment.

Tired of going to bars where the owner pays extra to keep a license for the patrons to smoke inside the establishment?

Tired of going to your favorite techno polka rave concerts, coming home smelling like an ashtray?

Tired of visiting a friend's vault, only to find out your friend refuses to use a designated, neighborhood Smoke Shack?

If you answered yes, consumer, then Spray on Selly is

for you! The product comes in 5 different designs. So easy, a lab monkey with only a pinky and thumb can use it.

(Believe us, we've made the necessary tests to prove our point.)

Just hold it 5 inches away, and spray.

Easy Peasy!

Check out our best review so far:

"What is so cool about Spray on Selly you can look like that character Selywn from the Multi-Colored Positronic Brain Waves. So much better, rather than purchasing a plastic costume, right?

"There's so many different options! Make an adjustment on the dial on the canister to wear a Selly suit, exactly how he looks in the book. Spin the dial and wear the one where his face was almost chewed off by that werewolf. Another adjustment and become Selwyn when he was mutilated, but saved from death by that dark guy.

"The best one, I think, is the adjustment for a drug-induced Selly. I mean, what better what hiding your own narcotic trip when you walk around in public?"

Don't waste another minute! Jack into your console, surf the Gridd, locate our 'site and order your own Spray on Selly today! And to make the deal sweeter the first 100 customers will receive a Bodykredd gift card valued at 50 bits to use at "The Joke's on You, Fella!" online store.

Order yours today!!

*This has been an approved message from the Dibbuk, Inc. ™

GIFTED

Twenty feet from the protective shield he swung once more before his feet hit the ground, leaving the playground and the other children. Roaming eyes always looked at him weird. Like he didn't belong in their group.

His best friend Tommy hadn't been like that before, why now? Why did it have to always happen when he friended another kid?

Mom called for him again.

Uncle Anders manned the grill, flipping vegan burgers. He gave the boy a wink and a reveal of wet, synthetic chewing tobacco tucked in the corner of his smile. He even shared the holographic yard gnomes on his apron the boy hated. Blink once, they struck a pose. Blink twice, they changed their pose. Blink again, they beamed and waved.

He used his pocket disintegrator-integrator to teleport to the porch.

"Joey! You scared me! Like one of those ghosts!"

"Sorry, Aunt Cecelia."

"That's okay." She grinned; tousled his hair. "I should know ghosts never leave their realm anymore, since Slader Corp banned them. Wished Weather Vane didn't have a malfunction. It'd be able to close the arctic space between this porch and the playground. If Tommy was here, he'd be able to fix it in a snap." Aunt Cecelia glanced at one of the kids. "Gods-rest-his-soul."

"Amen." Mom ate a forkful of food off her plate.

Cecelia drew a long drag from her pipe stem, blowing morphed smoke shapes, alien mimics from the pre-Shift Atari game *Space Invaders*.

It'd be cool to smoke a pipe and blow out aliens, the boy thought. *Maybe I could do that when I grow up. Wonder if you could blow out dragons, too?*

She winked. "What a handsome young man you have, Tracy. I can sense the 'Gift'."

"Yes. He'll be back. I'm sure of it. He'll return to us and be all grown up. Gonna be a popular with the girls."

"Yuck! I don't like girls!"

The women's laughter caused a smile on his father's face as he took a seat. "Good thing he's not into girls right now. We'd be in serious trouble."

Another laugh.

The boy sat by his mom. *I'm gonna miss mom and dad. Gonna miss waking up to the smell of blueberry pancakes, hearing mom argue with the Jolt maker to make a single cup of hot cocoa, since the coffee machine is always infected with the Tourette's Syndrome virus.*

Dad chuckling at mom's rant, assuring her he'd down-load the anti-virus to fix the issue later in the day. Funny thing was, dad seemed to always have an excuse for not taking care of it. Maybe dad enjoyed watching seeing mom blow raspberries, point her finger at some-thing she couldn't punish by grounding it for a week or make stand in a corner.

The boy giggled.

"What's so funny?" Mom smiled.

"Uh…nothing. Thinking about a joke I heard."

"Would you like to share it? Bet it's a good one."

Uncle Leroy and Aunt Betty stepped onto the porch, each carrying a plate of food.

"Well…" The boy frowned, playing it off. "Can't remember exactly how it goes."

"Oh. Well, if you can remember it after a while, please share it."

"Will do, mom."

"I love to hear jokes. So, does your Uncle Leroy," Aunt Betty's words fought to be heard around a mouthful of corn from the cob. Seconds before the flakes and juice dripped off her chin a black swarm escaped from behind her ear, consumed the food parti-cles, scurried back to point.

The boy gasped. Not a fan of flesh-cleaning Tidy-bots. Eerie to watch servos crawl the skin, searching for food waste. Sure, he could shove the disgusting bits and pieces of food perched on Aunt Betty's lips and chin rather than witness the swarm raping her flesh. Least they didn't leave red marks and did their job. His Dad once mentioned mankind had gotten bitten by the Lazy Bug. It made the boy think of a large bug kicked back in a recliner using its antennae to receive transmission from the wall vid.

Aunt Cecelia blew out a few more aliens. "Sure, can't knock Weather Vane. Good it was at a discount on the Gridd. Looks darn close to the real sun. Bright. Warm. Gives us a climate-controlled area. No need to bundle up in our snow suits. The processor does well, I think." She scratched her nose. "Something I miss. The actual sun."

"You still get to see it, Cecelia." Dad wiped his face with a napkin.

"You and your napkins," Mom snorted.

Dad shrugged. "I'm old school."

Mom's own Tidybots snatched a sliver of vegan burger below her lower lip.

This made the boy inch away from his mother. *Shouldn't be so creeped out by those things,* he thought. *You have a job to do. Remember, you are the Gifted one.*

"Only way to get a bird's eye view of the sun is peeking through my frosted windows, Frank," Aunt Cecelia said. "I wish to feel its warmth on my face again. I wish I could walk my dog. Thank goodness for Pooper Scooper bots." Chuckle. "Otherwise our solitude in our domes in this colony would stink." She gazed at nothing. "Probably wishing for a miracle, anyway."

Frank nodded, took another bite of his vegan burger, used his napkin.

"Our only miracle will be ridding those things out there in the snow." Aunt Betty said.

Frank swallowed. "Hard to believe they exist in the freezing cold."

"Doesn't surprise me. Their bodies don't have an ounce of feeling; only hate." Mom wrapped an arm around Joey, pulled him close.

Wish I didn't have to go. Wish I didn't have the stupid 'Gift'. Wished I could stay here and have blueberry pancakes every morning and read issues of Sellywn MacWith The Kung Fu Grip comics on my Recog tablet and play with other kids in the colony.

Am I ready to do this?

Goosebumps crawled the boy's neck. Fear tapped his spine.

Do I have what it takes?

Frank swallowed. "Those things out there changed the world. We were some of the lucky ones to survive. Thank goodness, we are still part of Ozarium. Otherwise we wouldn't be here right now."

"Maximus Slader is a saint. He was happy to yield to our wishes, setting us away from the hustle and bustle of Ozarium, developing this subsidiary colony. Being countryside is much better, but I don't blame him for our never ending snow. Slader can't control the weather. I blame that evil creature. Think he could have moved on by now?" Aunt Betty's cleaner bots consumed more flakes of corn.

"I'm sure he's still out there, waiting for us." Frank said. "He's still controlling his followers."

"Think he'd be done terrorizing and move on."

Dad shrugged. "According to Slader he has his demi agents working on it."

"Gods help us all if that creature isn't stopped!"

Uncle Leroy's bib overalls with animated dancing iguanas in Bermuda shorts snatched bits of food before his own Tidybots could take chase. The swarm acted confused, twitching on Leroy's chin. He laughed. "That tickles." The servos scurried before he could scratch. "Got my own cleaners." He pointed a meaty digit. "My iguanas are lightin' fast!" Guffaw.

"Oh, Leroy! You're so silly." Aunt Betty slapped him on the arm, chuckled.

Mom, Dad and Aunt Cecilia laughed as well.

Wasn't that *funny*, the boy thought. *Guess you have to be an adult to understand goofy nonsense. Too bad I couldn't come up with a joke which would've been funnier.*

Uncle Mike and Aunt Sara stepped on the porch, each carrying a plate of food. Uncle Mike was cool. He owned pre-Shift comics and movies, all available on the Recog, and shared the files with Joey.

"What's up, Joey?"

"Hey, Uncle Mike," Joey replied.

"Hello, my best nephew in the whole wide world!" Aunt Sara said.

"Hello, my best aunt in the whole wide world!" Joey replied.

"Hey! That's not fair!" Aunt Betty said, spitting out bits and pieces of a chewed up beet, her turn to confuse the Tidybots, spread in six different directions. "What about me and your Uncle Leroy? Aren't *we* the best, too?"

"Sure. All of you are the best!" Joey assured.

"Awwww! I know you do, honey!" Aunt Betty cooed, scratched Joey's head. "Don't worry, I'm only messin' with you!"

"Oh, leave the boy alone," Uncle Leroy chuckled. "Remember, he's 'Gifted', you know. Don't want to upset him. Might make him mad at us!" He scowled, cut the air with his plastic knife.

The adults laughed.

"Stop it, Leroy!" Aunt Betty continued laughing. "He'll be just fine! He ain't gonna get mad at us! We're family!"

Uncle Leroy leaned close, whispered in her ear.

Aunt Betty giggled, she flushed.

"Now, now, you two!" Aunt Cecilia said, pointing her pipe's stem, "this boy's too young to hear things like that. You'll cripple his mind before he's fourteen years old."

"He couldn't hear what I said. Right, Joey?"

Joey shook his head.

"See? Even if he heard it he wouldn't know no better." Uncle Leroy chewed off a bite of chicken flesh from the bone.

Aunt Cecilia furrowed her eyebrows, opened her mouth, but Mom cut her off: "Look, Frank! Isn't that your brother?"

"Sure is." Dad grinned. "Guess he got our message

after all and used his pocket disintegrator-integrator to teleport here. Must be telling Uncle Anders a joke. The guy's belly is jiggling so much, his gnomes are having trouble staying posed."

Mom frowned. "He desperately needs a shave."

"And a haircut," Aunt Cecelia added.

"Why does he insist on looking like that?" Mom's expression looked as if someone had stuck a dirty sock in her face.

Dad shot the women a Look. "Don't be mean. He's has been through a lot. Just because his appearance isn't the best, you need to remember what he did for us. He was the first Gifted one. He has to stay off the radar, you know. That creature out there can track down the ones who've survived. My brother has become a marked man. He has to keep the Clandestine chip under his skin so they won't track him."

"They have operations, you know," Aunt Cecelia said.

"Pardon?" Frank asked.

"Remember Tommy? Gods-rest-his-soul."

A chorus of Ah-men's from the adults, this time each squeezing their eyes shut, each with their palm in the air, a straight direct to the globe overhead depicting a fake of the four hooded gods residing in their own transparent sphere.

"Poor Tommy. Visiting the colony's One Stop Shop Medic wasn't good enough, morphing his face."

"Please don't bring that up, Cecelia," Mom frowned. "Why'd Tommy pick a clown face? Was he doing it as a joke? Look! I got goose bumps on my arm just thinking about it!"

"Least his clown face smiled."

"Didn't help matters, Leroy. Tommy was always an odd kid. Gods-rest-his-soul."

Another round of Ah-men's.

"Your brother darn near looks like he's a mountain man," Uncle Leroy stuck the three points of his plastic utensil. "You'd think he lived in the woods."

"And this is different from our garage?" Aunt Betty said. "It could easily be converted into woodland area. It's never clean. Why don't you agree to spend the extra BodyKredd and get a Butler?"

"Betty, Butler bots are overpriced. I want to use the money for something else."

"Such as?"

Hesitation, before replying: "Books."

Multiple pairs of eyes swarmed the guy in bib overalls. Even Joey.

"Your brain screwed on backwards? You've heard of the Montag No-Paperback Law. We'd be in serious trouble, Leroy. We may be a smaller, subsidiary colony on the outskirts of Ozarium—stuck out in the cold no less —but Slader Corp wouldn't hesitate sending the demi to snatch us from our home. They'd pay a visit to everyone here in their halftracks and place us all in handcuffs."

Speechless, Uncle Leroy shrugged, stuck a fork full of food in his mouth.

Mom cleared her throat. "Joey, you remember Johnny, don't you?"

Joey pondered. Shook his head.

"That's, your Uncle Johnny, dear," Mom told Joey. "He hasn't seen you since you were born. He's been in isolation."

Joey studied the tall guy. Stocky build. White beard. Long hair tied back in a ponytail.

Johnny shook Dad's and Leroy's hand, gave the women hugs, and Joey's introduction came last.

Uncle Johnny bent down on one knee. "Great to meet another Gifted one, Joey. I wish I could have met you a long time ago. When you were born I still lived among them, trying to find ways to rid them from the land. Back then my Dibbik suit didn't have the bells and whistles you'll have. I wish you the very best, kid. Being the Gifted one is a high honor."

Joey smiled. *Uncle Johnny was groovatronic! He's in the same league as Uncle Mike!*

Weather Vane's scheduled timer gravitated the sun westward, allowing the moon to materialize. Neon glinted off the group's Evo helmets as starbursts flooded their vision teleporting their minds into the virtual game *Hangman's Revenge* on the Quasi-Cinematix console. The game consisted of players taking turns sticking their neck in the noose before the executioner pulled the lever, tightening the rope, dropping the player through the trap door. The game also came with a "Quick Dread" option. The losing player grasping a one to ten second dread of suffocation when dangling.

A few adult drinks later with a slice of conversation – Joey drinking non-carbonated Grape Explosion from his favorite glass depicting holographic pics of badgers cartwheeling – a conglomerate of relatives stood behind him at the basement door inside his Dome.

Dad grinned. "Now, son, when you go down there, make us very proud. Remember, you *are* the 'Gifted' one."

"Don't be scared," Mom kissed his forehead. "Be strong."

"Gonna be just fine." Uncle Mike winked. So, did the gnomes.

"Sure will, kiddo," Uncle Leroy said, showing off a chocolate cake smudge on his front tooth. Unfortunately, Tidybots were forbidden to enter the mouth.

Uncle Johnny opened held a rectangular box, a blue light bounced back and forth across the cover. "Go ahead, open it, kiddo."

Joey grabbed the object inside. Heavy in his grasp. His reflection of awe in the chrome.

The basement door spiraled open. "Down there you'll find the replica," Uncle Johnny said. "Don't be scared. Remember, it's a fake; won't harm you. Speak to it. See how it acts. That way, you can study it before you leave."

A chill congealed a hard lump in Joey's throat.

"If it gets too much, push on its chest to switch it off. We use the units for a crash course before Gifted ones are sent out in the snow. A long time ago we found out how dangerous it was sending adults to fight. Masking themselves wearing a Dibbik suit did no good. The creatures spotted them immediately. Slaughtered them where they stood. Did not help the fact we are too tall for the quest. That's why children are the best defense.

"Be sure to choose the nebulous option once you don the suit. Blurring the suit's surface will prevent harm from those creatures. You'll look like them. Long as they do not find out who you are, you'll be safe. Blend in. Live amongst them. Study their ways until finally reaching the point of return. Don't do as I did. Trying to kill one made me a marked man. When you out grow out of the suit it is imperative to return to the colony. We have faith in you. We love you very much, kid."

All the adults smiled.

The rank of being Gifted made Joey beam. Confidence swelled.

"Be aware if they find out who you are, not like them, the master will possess you. I won't candy-coat it, Joey. I've seen it first-hand. You are of age and the one who can help us survive. While there is faith in Maximus Slader coming to our rescue," he glanced over his shoulder at the others, "I have to say I do not believe it to be so. I think he has left us to die. Joey, if DeFlect fails, we all die. Good luck."

The door spiraled shut. Joey descended with gooseflesh. His nose filled with mom and dad's scent after their embrace; his aunt's and uncle's lingered, especially Uncle Johnny's until stopping on the fifth from last step.

He cocked his head.

A whirr of a mechanism.

She sat on the edge of a cot waiting for him, a grin of hard plastic teeth.

"I am here to kill you, Joey." A series of beeps emanated from the replica child's skull. "Unless you join us." Her foot touched the floor. "There is much to learn living among us."

Joey gripped the harmonic pulse, Uncle Johnny gift.

The machine stepped forward.

"You will fit in, like so many others birthed before you during the days of the slaughter, the pre-Shift era. Master came," she stepped another foot forward, "saved us all by leading us into victory, killing the adults."

Joey grabbed the stair's railing.

"Much to learn within our group. Join us." Another step, more whirrs, the synthetic flesh below its right eye twitched. "Much knowledge to learn."

Joey backed onto the first step. *Could he return to see his mom and dad? Would they ignore his shouts and pleas if he ran back upstairs and pounded on the door?*

A blank stare. "Do not be afraid," a monotone voice scraped away the girl's. "Sensors indicate your fear. This is only a teaching model. Do not be afraid."

Joey's lump in his throat enlarged.

"I am programmed to be the victim. Do not fear me. Asimov Law states no harm to humans."

Joey let go of the railing.

The blank stare dropped. Synthetic flesh repeated the twitch. "You will love our ways," the girl's voice returned. "You will love the cold. Come," she reached out a hand, "allow me to show you what you have missed for so long. Adults are the root of evil. Children are the future."

Joey reached, though shoved the bot's chest, shutting it off. He did not wish to hear it anymore. If he intended to be the Gifted one, he should not be scared. *They* should fear *him*.

He donned the Dibbik suit. Stuck a plug in his ear.

"Hello. I am Vodburrk," the computer said. "I am at your service. Please direct any questions concerning this suit's model and directions of use to me. Would you like to get started?"

"Yes." Joey's said.

"Choose an option." Holographic words scrolled in front of his eyes. Multiple choices indicated how the suit worked, choices of climate control to food sources were listed. A few selections, such as Jet Pack or Amphibious, were not available with this model.

"To order more selections, please visit www.dibbik.-griddsurf. BodyKredd or finance plans are avail–"

A hand fell on his shoulder.

The head slumped on its shoulder, the chords in the neck stretched. A blank stare and the skin under its eye twitched. The lips did not move. "My master seeks revenge, Joey," the bot sent telepathic signals, "Your parents are not safe. Your relative's existence will be discontinued. The colony will be in distress. Uncle Leroy will pray for death after we remove his eyes. Aunt Betty's Tidybots will fail cleaning her blood. Your mom and dad will watch each other being skinned alive."

Joey glanced over her shoulder.

"No. You cannot return. You are in exile from the Danse-Rick colony. You cannot return. The choice of growing older has been eliminated. You will endure death. Unless you join us, bringing you into the fold of the wings, making you a matured child.

"Join us, Joey, less you'd like to feel the point of the wood shoved through your poop shooter," giggle, "as we hoisted upright, watch as you feel every little teensy weensy pain inside your flesh.

The door spiraled open. Joey stumbled into the thick snow. The door shutout the girl's wide, plastic smile, but not her giggles. "Think I'll pay a visit to your folks upstairs."

Joey hammered on the door with his fists, shouting for his mom and dad.

No response arrived.

Time passed, the snow layering him shrouds of white.

The frozen land gave no relief. Elevated snowdrifts and snow dunes made the venture treacherous. At one point, Joey's fear of being lost arrived. View of the door had long since collapsed with the wall of the howling snow. Any hope of following his footpaths back the way he traipsed dissolved.

Hours later Joey crested a rise. Beyond, a group

huddled together, circled around a tall figure. Checking his Dibbik suit's camouflage he descended.

The wind whipped against frozen bodies, small and large, high above the group. Horrid expressions masked snow covered faces, frozen in time during their impalements.

A lump of Dibbik suits congealed at the bottom of the wooden poles.

A small hand grabbed Joey's. A clown's face grinned. "Howdy! Wanna play with us?"

THE U PIKE

A *t this time all colonists should be on the way or at home. Weather Vane will reboot tomorrow at 5 am. A sun will brighten the sky; no rain involved in the forecast. Thank you so much for your cooperation, obeying Curfew. Remember: Trans-Merrick Corp is always concerned for your safety.*

Have a good night.

I could only wish for a good night ahead after receiving the transmission to my telecommunication chip in my head as I rocketed down an empty street in suburbia, my right hand gunning the bike's throttle.

Hopping over 2 blocks, taking a hard right, I braked.

An armored halftrack crawled, 2 armed demi agents on the back, scouting.

I detoured down a different street, passed houses. Pockets of orange lights glowed behind windows. Residents who were home, safe from being seen by the demi. Street lamps illuminated the streets, casting more dim than bright. Pre-war vehicles parked against the curbs, those small compact ones. And when I passed one lawn multiple red eyes followed me. An animated floating sign near the moving sidewalk indicated:

Hire Your Own clan of Servo Selly's To Pose On your Lawn Today! Each a servo Replica from the Netflix 5.0 Show Multi-Colored Positrons Brain Waves!

Another 3 blocks and my view was another crawling halftrack. The only way I could elude authorities was taking the U-Pike. Forbidden for colonists to travel, though my only escape home.

I hopped over more streets, accelerated, whipped through a transparent blinking red skull-faced emoji warning me to turn back immediately and slipped onto the U-Pike. The current of the river hung on my left; a long stretch of a concrete wall hiding the colony shouldered my left. Shoving the bike up and over a hill my descent quickened, then crested a second hill. My venture would complete an actual U shape around the colony. I could slip through another warning sign, hop two streets, end at home. Quickly. And the only advantage in my pocket would be authorities too busy scouring inside suburbia, not outside on the U-Pike.

Careening, shooting toward my destination which would detour me to the back porch of my dome, a freedom I hoped for, blindsided me.

One second I was speeding toward freedom; the

next, the world upended. I gasped, flailing my arms and hands, crashing head-first onto the pavement. If not for my helmet, it would have resulted in a cranium split. However, the CPU in my safety suit failed to ignite its crash feature, expanding with foam as a cushion, preventing my bones being crushed.

Somehow, I was lucky. I could actually move, and peeled myself from the road. I my right leg folded and I fell back; my vision a darkened sky.

And ghostly faces.

I opened my mouth to form a word, choked down a tasteless spray, as my body became numb. Neurotransmitters in my brain inform me authorities had caught me, though the ghostly faces under the dark hoods refreshed me otherwise.

My last sight before darkness beckoned: my bike upside down, the front wheel spinning, oil bleeding on the road.

My eyes fluttered open, a shimmer of vision until my eyes adjusted.

My limbs forbid any movement from the neck down, no matter how hard I struggled under the leather straps in an upright box with a window at the head. A constant sting, though small, lay in the bend of my arm. An IV line filled with a blue liquid snaked through a tiny hole and connected to 1 of the 3 bags of more colored liquid hanging on a metal stand outside.

I blinked; swallowed saliva down a dry throat full of razors.

I ruled out the possibility of lying inside a One Stop Shop Medical facility; med bots with fat heads and long antennas working in a sterilized chrome room. The place resembled a bedroom in someone's dome.

Fighting to move caused pain. Chills crawled my flesh.

Questions of why was I here and not at the mercy of a med bot was unknown. Who's responsible for placing me here? Those ghost faces? An attempt to use my interface app in my brain to call my parents only received static. More attempts were defunct.

More chills crawled my skin, shoving me back into a darkness which welcomed me back, open arms.

∾

Voices.

Through the box's window I saw a dark-haired woman speaking to two men in business suits. I heard her say "blood", "specimen", "he'll get better", "the medicine he's receiving prevents dehydration", and "feed time". Other words were spoken, though garbled.

"Specimen" and "feed time" had me confused, but I supposed the others made sense.

I opened my mouth to try and speak, but another slice of the razors prevented it. The more I watched the three chat, even catching the woman's head turn in my direction, my eyelids grew heavy and I drifted back asleep.

A tasteful aroma woke me up. Reminded me of my mom's quick nuke of pork chops prepared in the Food Processor Turbo. Excitement diminished as the present reminded me where I lay. The small window in the box had lifted and I stared at the ceiling. Dark curtains blocked out most of the artificial sunlight from the window cut into the ceiling, except for the peeking orange around the fabric.

The dark-haired woman sat at my bedside.

Groggy, I stared at her.

She smiled.

"Eat, honey." Her tone almost sounded like my mom's, that time I was sick in bed.

A forkful of delicious food deposited into my mouth. Chewing wasn't easy, as if I needed to relearn the motions all over again. Chicken broth ran down my chin and she used the corner of a napkin to wipe.

My stomach grumbled. When had I ate last?

The woman wiped another spot of broth away. "Chew slowly, then swallow."

The razors in my throat changed into sandpaper. Soon it smoothed out, returning to the norm, soiled with saliva.

"Good boy." She smiled, a lock of her hair fell in front of her eyes. "You need your strength. You need to be big and strong again, young man." She giggled, lightly touched the tip of my nose with her finger.

It was at that time I noticed something rather odd as she said spoke those words. I was surprised I hadn't seen it before, when she had first smiled, her lips parting slightly. A chill snaked down my spine.

I thought maybe my eyes were playing tricks on me or something. I blinked a few times, not knowing for sure, but the way I was feeling at the time, groggy, my brain cloudy, anything could have been possible. I think if an apparition of a polka-dotted elephant wearing a helmet sitting on a tricycle juggling pink tennis balls appeared at my bedside, it would not have shocked me in the least.

Still, I wished that I had known where I was.

"Eat, honey. Good boy."

As time continued its crawl it made me wonder what day it was or how many weeks— even months—had gone by. The curtains shielding the artificial light stayed drawn, the orange peeking around the edges from time to time. I was awakened periodically by the dark-haired woman's voice and fed tasty meals. Besides chicken, a generous portion of salmon, trout, turkey, sweet potatoes, kale greens, and other vegetables were fed to me. Everything was delicious. I think that my stomach would actually rumble when I heard her say: "Hello, my little man, time to eat!" I almost felt as if I was in Heaven. All the food I wanted; all the rest that I could ever desire; all the comforts of being taken care of. Part of me enjoyed it. The food, the attention this woman was giving to some geeky twelve-year old who loved to watch horror and sci-fi vids and read digital comics about my favorite superhero Kilgor Traft warmed my heart. However, the other part of me felt the dread of never being able to get out of bed to walk, run, ride my bike, use the bathroom by myself without the woman holding my private part so I can urinate in a plastic urinal (very embarrassing) or ever again have the energy to lift a finger to feed and take care of myself.

I also missed my teaching bot and caregiver, Pete. He was all I had after being orphaned three years ago when my parents had died in the crash.

I became depressed.

No more swimming with my friends. No more visiting the ice cream shop. No more climbing the hill to sneaking a peek at R-rated movies the pre-war drive-in offered to adult viewers late Friday and Saturday night.

Destined to be forever a cripple, there was nothing I could do, except lay in this bed until dumped into my grave.

At times, I actually wished for it.

One day, I woke hearing many different voices. A crowd of dressed up people stood inside the room talking to one another. It was a party of some sort. I could smell something delicious and my eyes could see a buffet of food laid out on a long table against a wall.

Everyone held wine glasses full of something crimson in color.

My stomach rumbled.

The dark-haired woman made chatted with a few men. She was laughing and it must have been contagious, because nearly everyone else in the room enjoyed her words. Except me. I could not hear them.

I noticed that my left arm draped over the edge of the box. The IV was still stuck in the bend of my arm and no longer connected to a bag. It connected to a chrome contraption which was round in diameter, the width of a miniature beer keg, sitting on its own four legs.

The IV line filled with my blood.

A heavyset man stepped forward, bent down on one knee, pulled back his lips, showing a rack of pointy teeth. Then stood, gripping a wine glass of my blood.

This bizarre object was sucking out my blood!

I wanted to scream, but couldn't muster enough energy to do so.

"Cheers, young one!" the man said after taking a drink, holding out his glass, showing me his blood-stained shark-like teeth. These people, or whatever mutant monstrosities they were, had fed and fattened me up like a pig for a pig roast. Thoughts of roasting over an open fire came to mind.

Everyone in the room heard the man speak to me and now stood at my box. Or, perhaps, my coffin.

"Cheers!" They raised their glasses.

Fear uncoiled like a snake inside my gut.

"Cheers!" They lifted their lips, showing their sharp racks of teeth.

All of them were very happy, holding their glasses, my blood in their stomachs.

My dark-haired caretaker stood at the foot of my coffin and raised her glass as well, smiling from ear to ear.

Fighting to get up and run was useless. Fighting to scream was useless. And fighting to stay awake much longer depleted my energy, as darkness cackled and took hold of my hand.

But not before the contraption whirred and clicked and morphed and grew two antennas for eyes, gazing at me through snowy lenses, as if they were miniature vid screens. Six metal legs grew out of its side and it released itself from its base.

The crowd moved out of its way to give it a clear path.

The IV line trailed behind, a long strip of blood.

Then the group all laughed, leaving it the last I heard as the world upended and I spiraled down into a pitch-black tunnel.

And that was when I could scream.

As time played its horrifying games, I was fed and bled. I was given the nourishment of both carbohydrates and protein so they could drain me, milking me for their pleasure. For their parties. For a snack. The blood-sucking shiny contraption never missed a visit to their get togethers. Sharp fangs and giggles and laughter and toasts to me continued over and over as they repeated: "Cheers, young one!" Sometimes the faces were different; other times they were familiar, as if I was shared amongst a group of blood-drinking monstrosities.

I was their prisoner, the giver of their drink.

At one point I wondered if they would eventually slaughter and eat me. That would be the encore for the audience to swallow, right?

My gut-feeling told me that I would never see the outside world again. Ever. This room had become my tomb.

That was when I knew I had to find a way to escape.

One morning I woke up staring at the curtained window and the artificial sunlight. I felt somewhat better. My brain not so much stuffed in the clouds. The IV bottle had run dry and the line had a small sliver of blood congealed inside. Without the fluid, it had nowhere else to go. The IV needle had vanished. In its place was a large bandage.

I happened to notice the door to my room was shut and a slice of light appeared at the bottom.

I decided I to try get up. When I did, the world spun. And my back screamed along with it.

I laid back down, fighting back tears from the pain of the razor blades slicing through my spine.

The pain eased up.

The lower half of my body would not budge. I was paralyzed from the waist down. Wincing, realizing a soreness where the IV needle had been stuck, I fought to sit up, which took longer than it had because used the edges of the coffin as leverage. Somewhere beneath the skin a razor blade twisted into my spine.

I bit my bottom lip and tears drained down my cheeks.

Sucking in a deep breath, blowing it out, undergoing more pain than I could possibly imagine, I slid off the bed and onto the floor with a hard thump.

I thought for sure my spine would rip itself out of my skin when I heard my vertebrae pop and crack.

Through tears, I used my fingertips and fingernails to gain purchase on the hardwood floor as I crawled, towing one big lump of numb flesh consisting of two legs and a torso.

A shadow blocked out the light under the door.

I froze, laying there wondering if I could make it back to my bed or not, actually climbing back inside the coffin.

I heard voices behind the door.

I started crawling back towards the coffin, pain continuing to be my best and only friend, and reached the edge to pull myself back up.

I heard the doorknob twist.

I attempted to climb head-first into the casket.

The doorknob twisted again and the latch clicked.

Frantic, sweating, and wanting to cry and scream

from the pain slicing through my body, I started slipping backward. I bit back a cry and tasted blood as I bit my bottom lip again.

The fall wasn't as bad I thought, though the pain still hung around.

I lay there breathing heavily, wishing for relief from the pain. I braced myself, knowing when the door swung wide, I would see her and a few of her men.

Time passed.

The door stayed shut.

The pain slowly subsided.

So, I tried again. What did I have to lose? Returning me to my coffin? Bleeding me over and over again?

I managed to crawl to the door, stretch to grasp the doorknob, and give it a twist. A big surprise to me, the door unlatched, revealing a long stretch of a hall made up with mirrors. Recessed lights blazed from above. A single door sat at the end, red in color.

I crawled, heading for the door. I knew the chance of it being an exit could possibly be nil, but I hoped for a strong chance I was wrong. Hell, I prayed I was wrong.

Behind the mirrors I heard sobbing. Another few crawls and I heard giggles. Who was behind there? More prisoners like me? If that was the case, I wanted to help them, but in my state, how could I? I had to save myself.

The constant fear those doors swinging open and the dark-haired woman or any of the others showing up chilled me. They would surely drag me back to my room, chanting "Cheers, young one!"

Surprisingly, nothing happened.

And the further I crawled, the more the hallway seemed endless, as if it grew after my grip on the floor. Each side appeared like a funhouse mirror. Either my slithering frame would become fat, thin, short, or stumpy.

I heard a low hum, much like a machine in a factory.

The volume rose, whirrs and clicks and a pop, lifting hairs on my neck, sending goosebumps across my skin. A vibration snaked along my spine.

The sound continued rising, now drilling into my temples, causing my head to explode with pain. I stopped moving, squeezed my eyes shut, covered my ears, hoping to hold shove away the sound.

It didn't help.

The sound washed over me like a wave.

God knows I tried to shove it out of my head. I wanted to shout for my mom, only to find I could not produce the words. My jaw felt wired shut. My joints felt as if worms writhed inside. My bones felt as if they would shatter. I prayed for the pain to leave; but it did no such thing, only escalated.

At one point I screamed.

The sound of door creaked open.

Raising my eyelids, slits to peek through, dark figures approached and loomed over my frame. Ghostly faces gazed with bright, yellow eyes. Their bleached white skin stretched over their skull faces. They showed me their fangs.

And giggled.

Pinpricks spread over me. I wished it were a hallucination; but, it was not.

Crawling across my body small robotic spiders whirred and squeaked, quickly bounding me in a large cocoon of their web. A few scurried close to my eyes, twitching their tiny fangs.

I passed out.

I woke up inside my coffin. The terrible pain had vanished. So, had the weird-looking ghost-faced creatures and the spiders. The IV had been slipped back into my vein and the IV bag had been refilled. I also noticed the bend in my arm wasn't hurting. For some reason I felt good. If I could move my legs I could run ten miles or hop on my bike and cruise.

My mind switched gears. My thoughts turned to the great care I was receiving: good food; rest; and good friends.

And as I write this, another party has started. It's a party for me. My return to the coffin. Everyone in the room is smiling. Even my favorite dark-haired woman who feeds me every day. Thinking about the delicious food makes my mouth water.

They have told me how happy they were I stayed. Why would I ever think about leaving? You have everything you would ever need, right here, with us. What would they ever do without me?

So very kind, they all are.

I've been told I'm going to be a live-in resident here for a very a long time. Healthy, young kids who are active, not the ones who sit in front of the television playing video games after school day in day out, are who they need to survive. Only blood.

All is good.

All is well.

The other day I could have sworn I caught a glimpse of my mom and dad at one of the parties drinking my blood, talking to the crowd, laughing, waving at me. Mom blew me a kiss. I love her and dad and I guess now I'll never be without them.

If they were actually alive, I'd had believed it.

As I look down, I notice a white patch growing across the top of my hand. And the more I notice, my arms are spotted as well.

My friends are saying its nothing to be worried about.

Could they be right?

DARK PLACES OF REST

PROLOGUE

A cold rainfall chased Tobias inside an old vacant building. Thunder boomed and lightning struck. Other buildings sat inside an enclosed area wrapped with chain-link fence.

"Thatch. You copy?"

A small black and white screen on the vintage Samsung cellphone snowed, eventually exposing a chubby face and a mop of long hair.

"Yeah," Thatch's voice crackled through the plastic grill. "I got ya. Make the trip okay, Tobe?"

"Yeah. I think that the churns are startin'. Can't talk very long."

"Understandable, bro. Look, I'll send you the file on that Limon."

"Cool."

An interception made the screen warble and bleed

snow, then return the chubby face. "…iller retrieved the info without any problems."

"Say that again, Thatch. Lost transmission."

"Oh. Sorry, dude. Friggin' time traveling transmits are always shit. I said, I will also send you the info about his living accommodations asap. Miller downloaded it. The guy's a wiz on the terminals."

"Good." Nausea showed its face; bile crawled up his throat.

"Miller said two more people bought the farm today. Poor souls. Most can't stand all of the hard work and heat up there on the surface. Especially me, my overweight lump in all. Those aliens have to be stopped soon. We can't keep this slavery crap up much longer."

"Well…" Tobias swallowed, a mistake forcing the bile from exposing itself. He burped up half-digested particles of this morning's breakfast. "This new idea of time travel and targeting the cause of the downfall of our Earth might work. Miller best be right about doing this. Otherwise, we are shit out of luck."

"I know. Hey, is it raining there?"

"Yeah. Hear it? Coming down in sheets."

"Wow. We never have rain much anymore."

"Nope. Global warming extreme screwed everything up." Stomach acid joined with bile and flakes of this morning's breakfast made a crawl up his throat.

"Ever since those freaks popped out of the sky, the entire atmosphere has been screwed. Never rains. Always a desert heat. Anyways, end of rant, take care of yourself, Tobias. I'm out."

"Later." The churns, a time traveler worst enemy, crashed into him and he hurled bile before he could pocket the Samsung.

Minutes later, wiping his mouth, he staggered outside, stood in the rain. He remembered a time when he hated it, now he welcomed it as it cascaded off his face.

Tobias pushed a button on his bracelet, morphing his black spandex outfit into a t-shirt, sweat shirt, a pair of jeans, shoes, and a thick jacket. A baseball cap sat atop his head.

His Samsung beeped.

Thatch sent the information about Limon. Staring at his picture, Limon looked completely normal. Weren't some serial killers like that? Wearing flesh to hide their terror?

Tobias received the location where to find this guy. He flipped up the collars on his jacket and set out in the pouring rain.

CHAPTER ONE

Limon sat the old black and white picture of the deceased down on the end table. A young man wrapped his arm around a young woman's waist. Both smiled, very happy together. Now her face had long erased the expression, lying in the open casket in the front of the room. Colorful flowers and wreaths posed on stands. A collage of snapshots from a Polaroid were stuck on a poster-size piece of card stock paper secured with a thin sheet of plastic. Photos depicted the dead woman's previous life full of happiness: laughing, smiling, vacationing on the beach, working in her garden wearing her favorite sunhat, and sitting on the couch opening Christmas presents.

The woman's life had been better than Limon's could ever be.

Sherry broke up with him six months ago, stating that she could not bear to live under the same roof as a mortician. Limon couldn't help it—well, I guess he *could*, but he didn't want to change jobs because the money was good. Plus, his father had been in the funeral business, and his father before that. The family tradition had been passed down from generation to generation, never a skip. And it was one of the things Limon knew how to do well: take care of the dead.

"Limon, where should we put these?"

"On that end table, Mark, by the small statue."

"Our visitors should be arriving soon." Mark sat the vase down.

"Yes." Limon looked at his watch. "In about an hour."

Hired no sooner than he could get his diploma from mortuary school Mark became an asset to Limon. The kid was a good worker and the only one in his family interested in the business.

"I'll be right back, Mark. I need to go downstairs for a minute."

"Sure thing."

Simon flipped a switch on the wall and the lights flickered twice before it bathed the floor below in is glow. In the center of the room sat two stainless steel porcelain embalming tables about five feet apart from each other. Two centrifugal pumps at the foot of a long counter were used to shove formaldehyde through the corpse's veins. Deep troughs ran along the perimeter of both tables, eliminating the need for a splash guard. At the foot was a drain where the fluids escaped into the sewer system.

Limon opened a door to a storage closet filled with

chemicals and tools needed for embalming and walked inside and to another door with a large padlock. He unlocked it. Darkness flooded the inside added with a musty aroma. Originally, the room had been used an extra storage room when his father had owned the funeral home.

Now it was used as Limon's special place.

With a pull of a string a light bulb brightened. Three coffins with a nice oak finish and brass rails sat in the room. Limon ran the tip of his finger slowly over the top before lifting the lid.

He smiled.

Blue eyes gazed at Limon, but they were as lifeless as his young body. Lips sutured shut, bruises plagued the man's face, as well as some that were around his neck where Limon had squeezed with both hands. Once they were unconscious, they were so much easier to embalm.

"Sorry, Michael. You just could not keep your nose out of other people's businesses. Could you?"

Michael's corpse said nothing.

"I did not want you to end up like this, my friend. You shouldn't have returned to work the other night. You wouldn't have seen that guy there," he pointed to the other coffin, "being worked on. You wouldn't have heard the guy scream all the way upstairs if I had muffled his mouth. What did you think you could do? Stop me?"

Michael said nothing.

"There was a chance you could've, my friend. Your

biggest mistake was taking your eyes off me while you punched in the number to the cops on your cellphone."

Limon frowned. "Maybe I could have handled our conversation differently. Maybe I could have talked you into doing the killings with me. There's a chance you would have liked it. Then again, perhaps not.

"One good thing that came from this, buddy. Now you get to see your folks. That's always a bonus for dying, right?"

Michael still did not respond.

"I might like that, when the time comes for me to die. It'd be good to see my father."Limon grinned.

"Anyway, tell your mom and dad 'Hi' for me. God bless."

Limon patted Michael's chest and closed the lid.

CHAPTER TWO

U nder a WELCOME TO ST. JUDAS sign a neon slit in the dark opened. A pulsing orb with a blended violet and red color appeared. A face materialized in the center, then grew, infecting the orb, shaping it into a floating head.

The slit in the dark sealed up, dissipated, as if it had never existed.

The floating head made its way to the closest house it could locate and gazed through a window.

Moving pictures from a television screen cascaded over a man and woman who sat cuddled together on a couch.

The floating head drifted behind the house, thinned itself out, and slithered under the door. Reshaped into a head it grew spider arms and scurried across the linoleum, onto the carpet, sliding behind the couch.

The head's eye stretched away from its socket on a

stalk, peeking at the two adults. Running a sequence, it found that the woman held a blue and green aura, while the man held a yellow and black.

The head chose its victim.

"Are you okay, hun?" the wife asked.

"I...just felt a terrible chill."

"Scared of the movie, dear?" His wife laughed.

"No. Heck no."

The floating head became a thin membrane and as sharp as a scalpel sliced the skin on back of the man's neck, invading his person, diving into old memories. Capturing his weaknesses, especially his battle with depression after losing his first wife in a car wreck.

The man rose, rubbed the back of his neck. Words formed, left his lips, "I'm getting a little hungry," but it was not his.

"Get me a Coke, would ya?" the woman asked.

"Sure."

The man observed himself walk into the kitchen, open a cabinet drawer, returned to the living room, finding it empty.

He heard the toilet flush.

Light splashed the hallway for a second as the woman emerged from the bathroom, then switched off. She followed the glow of the TV and sat down.

A hand covered her mouth and her screams were muffled as a sting ripped across her throat. The spray of blood splashed the hand as it returned to work its blade a second time.

She watched with her one good eye, the one still in use, as her husband climbed the stairs.

Her children's screams chased her into darkness.

CHAPTER THREE

The rain stopped.

Rocks crunched under Tobias' shoes as he walked under a bridge. Traffic crossed overhead. The chain on the gate wasn't a problem. Tobias' had it open within seconds by using a small tool.

Thunder rumbled across the skies, the sound reminding him of his past. If he could only padlock the door shut inside of his skull and not bring back the—

horror of the spacecraft thundering over Tobias while he sped home in the car. It was the first day of the genesis which morphed the world into death.

"Authorities are instructing people to find immediate shelter. If you have a basement or cellar, now is the time to hide. Outside is not safe," the radio announcer said. "The township of Riley Creek has been destroyed. The United States Air Force has deployed fighters and is said to be here within the hour."

Tobias turned onto a street, nearly sideswiping a

speeding vehicle.

People were everywhere. They ran from their houses carrying suitcases, carrying children, even small dogs, except for the one that ran in front of his car. Tobias swerved, crashed into a brick mailbox.

So much for everyone staying inside, he thought.

He threw the shifter into reverse.

When he pulled into his driveway his neighbor was backing out, spinning his tires and crashed into a parked car sitting across the street.

Jimmy from across the street flew out of his front door cursing.

The truck's transmission shifted into first the vehicle roared toward downtown.

The neighbor never once looked Tobias' way.

Or Jimmy who still cursed.

Tobias sprinted inside to get Katie. He couldn't leave without her. An explosion rocked the ground, shook the house, causing him to lose his balance. At least the comfort of his sofa caught his weight. Pictures of his mom and dad crashed the floor. The wooden cross of Jesus on the wall flipped upside down and hit the floor. The kitchen cabinet coughed out plates and bowls.

Tobias watched a billow of smoke rise not far off.

He scooped up the TV remote.

A slender, attractive woman stood in the park downtown. In the background, flames and black smoke rose three hundred feet behind her.

"It is mayhem down here! Buildings are on fire. People are dead."

The camera panned left, revealed truth to her words.

The flash of a memory when Tobias and Melissa lounged in a spot on the grass years ago, both laughing and teasing with each other, slid back into its groove. At that time the spot on was green, not covered with a body in flames.

Jenny pointed. "Over there, where the First Savings Bank sat, is in rubble. And over there is where the flower sh-"

A large shadow blocked the sun.

"Wow! Those space crafts are huge!"

The camera focused on the spacecraft before it gained momentum and blasted off.

"I'm not sure why that ship flew away. Maybe their done with us." Her eyes widened. "Um…oh, no."

A loud sound distorted the TV's speaker, blocked out the sun.

The newswoman dropped her microphone and ran.

But not before the blue heat ray made her body explode into red bits and pieces.

The screen went to snow.

"Jesus!" Tobias backed away from the TV, almost losing his balance. He ran upstairs, packed a few things in a duffle bag. Since Katie didn't move very quick, he grabbed her and ran out of the house, not bothering to lock the doors, or silencing the depression on TV where the shocked face of a man appeared on camera, manning the news desk.

Tobias' small engine revved as he spun out of the driveway, shifted gears, mashed the pedal and

busting through the front door when they were in their room in bed having s—

The last words he said to Madelyn while she was in the kitchen, before she stumbled into the living room, a strange expression on her face and her lips moving, trying to form words, only a grunt or murmur crawling from her throat.

Now the husband sat in front of the minister's words, listening, but not paying attention, while the husband's mind drifted elsewhere, still with his wife.

"—from Heaven and smiling," the minister continued. "It is her celebration to be with the Lord. No pain. No suffering. She has gone home. Brothers and sisters, there is only rest, with the Lord."

"Amen," a few people in the crowd say.

The husband's bottom lip quivered.

"Now, Bill," the minister directed his attention, "there will be days that you will wake up and look over at an empty space in your bed. Even if you are dreaming of running through a field, hand in hand with your wife, and thinking that as soon as the dream ends, you will find Madelyn by your side—but you won't."

Bill choked back a sob.

"There may be an empty chair by the fireplace that Madelyn used to sit in; an empty space in the kitchen where she made dinners; an empty space in your life." The minister paused. "Bill, do you know that there is no empty space in heaven? There, everything is reserved. One day you will visit Madelyn and a small table will be placed in the corner, reserved for the both of you to share. I assure you that your wife is in a better place and she loves you very much.

"Let us bow our heads, and pray. God, please take Madelyn into your arms and show her your love. Give her the love that you give to us. Give her a new life up in Heav-"

Bill cracked. He wailed, holding his head in his hands. The minister stepped away from the podium and held out his hand to touch Bill's shoulder.

Bill leaped to his feet, knocked the minister to the side, and ran to the casket. He grabbed one of Madelyn's hands, prying it away from the other.

"I love you so much, Madelyn! Come back to me!"

Mark looked at Limon, as if saying, what do we do?

Limon shook his head. "Stay here. We can't get in the middle of this."

The minister tried consoling Bill.

"Get away from me!" Bill spat and gave his dead wife's hand a yank.

It tore off.

"P-P-Please, Madelyn, come back to me!" Bill stammered, clutching the hand, kissing it. "Please, God, return her to me! I've never doubted you! I-I-I've always had faith in you, Lord! H-H-How can you do this t-t-to MEEEEE!"

By now most of the crowd were on their feet.

The minister tried again.

"Stay away from me! You loved to talk to her at church. On the phone at our house!"

"Bill, I was there to help her understand the Word of God," the minister defended.

"No! You were there to steal her away from me! You wanted to sleep with my *wife*!"

Awes and shocked faces ran through the mourners.

"Heavens no! What on earth why you would think that?"

"Because she loved chatting with you. She'd always talked about you. I got sick of it. *So freaking sick of it*!" punctuating each word.

"She wanted to learn more about the Bible, Bill. I taught her."

"You taught her how to ignore me. You taught her how to wreck our marriage by not wanting to be around me anymore. She used to tell me how bad of a person I was."

"Bill, I never said such a thing! I would never wreck your marriage."

"Well, *someone* told her lies. She only spoke to one other man than me before she died. Wonder who it could have been?" Bill glared at the minister.

The minister looked frightened. "Bill, you're upset. You're not thinking clearly."

"Oh? I'm not?"

"No. You've been under this terrible stress. The loss of your wife."

"Do me a favor, just stay the hell away from me."

"Bill…allow me to console you." The minister stepped forward.

"Keep your distance, preacher." Bill pressed his

wife's hand against his chest. "I don't need anybody." He looked at the crowd. "None of you people either! Screw you *all*!"

Gasps ran through the crowd.

"Get out, all of ya's!" Bill screamed. "I don't need you anymore!" He burst out crying, stumbled, fell on the floor.

Family members ran to him, tried to calm him, even his only son.

Bill curled up in a ball, clutched the hand, sobbed, mumbled: "Madelyn, please come back.... pleeeeasse!"

"Can't we do anything?" Mark asked.

"Let them handle it," Limon told him. By now family members calmed Bill down. He still held onto Madelyn's hand. No one could take it from him. Limon had seen a couple funerals like this. Some could be calm, good as gold; while some got out of hand. There was one funeral where two brothers got into a fist fight because they blamed each other for their mother's death. The casket was even knocked over and the glue that Limon had used to seal the corpse's eyes and mouth shut popped open. When that happened, the fighting stopped. The family called it an omen, actually believing the old woman's soul had returned to Earth, showing fury of displeasure toward her sons.

Bill's son helped him stand and they walked into the room where coffee and sandwiches lay. Bill still held Madelyn's hand, at least until his son coerced him into giving it up to be returned to the casket.

CHAPTER FIVE

"Today, we celebrate Madelyn McMyers going home," the minister expressed to a crowd of mourners.

Outside the rain fell in sheets, a thousand fingers drumming the roof of the funeral home.

The widowed husband wore a very sad, very pale face. The past few days had been rough for everyone, a surreal reality where one could not believe Death could had been so close by, close enough to grab the hand of a wife and kidnap her. One night the husband and wife were recollecting all their wonderful years of marriage: four daughters, two married off, the other two in college. All their hardships during the twenty-five years: financial troubles, the strike in 1950 at the factory costing not only employees problems but the company as well. Then the conversation switching gears: laughing about that one time when—

Giggling about when the neighbor's kid came

family by launching it into a lake. He started off toward town to locate his contact.

Let nothing stand in the way of his species taking over Earth by rooting out the population of the human race.

After everyone had left, the ghost of Bill's outburst lingered. The flowers and the wreaths stood there like statues, waiting to be gathered and taken home, or off to the burial site.

Limon flicked the light switch on the basement wall, descended the steps, unlocked his secret room, placed a body bag on the embalming table, unzipped and spread it wide. He placed Michael's corpse inside.

Limon rolled a gurney holding the corpse out the back door to his car.

CHAPTER SIX

T he kidnapper walked through the dark woods. A flickering red neon light shone just ahead. A local bar. Vehicles littered the parking lot. He needed a ride.

Noise inside of the bar leaked outside. People laughing, shouting. Country music blaring. A bottle smashed and someone wailed "*Whoooooweeee!*"

The kidnapper slid behind the wheel of an old Dodge, hot-wired it, and the engine sparked to life. He put it in gear, drove a half mile before switching the headlights on.

He pulled out a cell phone he stole from the family he murdered. He had converted it into his own communication device. He tapped open an app and a small hologram of a sphere materialized, glowing yellow, and spun.

He used his victim's vocal cords to speak.

"Arrived safe. Will find Zifir. Make sure the job is operated correctly."

The sphere pulsed bright yellow.

"I understand."

The sphere pulsed bright yellow twice.

"Yes. The one who arrives from the Rebellion will be killed."

This time the sphere flickered its yellowish red.

"Initiate Sequence 4 after mission is accomplished to return. Understood."

The Dodge cruised into the night.

CHAPTER SEVEN

Houses lined one side of the street; a river sat on the other. A car passed Tobias, then a truck with country music drifting out of the windows, a tune about a cheatin' woman.

Limon's house lay about a half mile off.

CHAPTER EIGHT

H eadlights sliced the darkness. Tires crunched gravel in the driveway leading to a very old church in front of a cemetery, the place where Madelyn's plot awaited her. Trees ran along each side; their trunks thick, limbs grown, stretched out.

The car rolled to a stop. The headlights shut off, the driver's side door opened, and Limon got out. He opened the trunk and pulled out the body bag, slung it over his shoulder, grabbed a flashlight. The blaze shoved darkness back as he walked over the spot where Madelyn's plot was. A canopy had been set up, covering it. The brass handles on Madelyn's casket would soon be hooked onto the railing and after a button was pushed the casket would lower into the grave while mourners stood by and watched as their loved one returned to the earth, ashes to ashes, dust to dust.

Jacob had done a good job. The old guy had a mean weapon for digging up the earth, his own backhoe and a shovel to boot. Limon had called him two days prior, explaining the details, and like usual, the guy followed through with his work. He made sure to indicate to Jacob the dimensions, especially leaving enough open space at the bottom by lying about the caskets starting to be thicker these days.

The old guy never questioned the job. He did what he was told to do.

Limon dropped Michael's body into the hole and went up to the church. There was a small shed out back. He used his light to find something. He returned to the burial plot, sat the flashlight on the ground, aimed the beam at the hole, and used the shovel to scoop dirt from the pile beside the plot. When he finished he had thrown about two feet of dirt on the body bag. When they lower the coffin, no one would ever know that another body lay underneath.

He gathered up the flashlight and returned the shovel to the shed and walked to his car. A young man lay in the trunk, unconscious, gagged, hands tied behind his back.

Limon grinned. He had scored another hitchhiker on the travel here.

He had pulled off onto the shoulder of the road, offered him ride. The guy accepted. Limon made small talk, like news and sports. Fifteen minutes later Limon complained he didn't have any brakes. There wasn't actually anything wrong with them, he faked it, and allowed the car to roll to a stop on the shoulder of the road in the middle of nowhere by easing off the accelerator. Acting as if he knew how to fix the problem, he pulled the lever to open up the hood. He told the guy he had tools in the trunk, so if the guy wanted to, he could just stay seated.

The guy said, "Cool."

Limon walked back to the trunk. He waited a few seconds, then asked the guy give him a hand with something. The boy was happy to help. Limon pretended he had trouble searching for his tool box and flashlight in the dark trunk. Plus, he lied about having issues with his hand going numb for no reason. Blaming a nerve problem stemming from his neck.

Limon asked if the guy minded reaching into the trunk to find the toolbox and flashlight.

The hitchhiker stretched his arm, reaching far. When he did, Limon slammed the head of a hammer into the guy's head.

Not once, but three times, making sure the guy was knocked.

Limon wanted him to sleep awhile. The hitchhiker needed his rest. The fun was about to begin.

CHAPTER NINE

The Dodge rolled to a T in the road.

Headlights splashed the windows of a house. A wooden fence wrapped the front yard and a Big Wheel and a bike with training wheels sat on the sidewalk leading to the front porch.

The kidnapper looked at his device. It indicated he was only two miles away. He turned the wheel, followed the road. A twenty-four-hour convenient store sat off to his right, and a woman stood there at the gas pump getting ready to fill her small car.

He should be at his destination very soon.

CHAPTER TEN

L imon stood over the naked hitchhiker strapped to the stainless-steel porcelain embalming table. The victim appeared to be a healthy and in good shape.

A pity for him to have to die.

He regained consciousness. Fear danced in his brown eyes. He tried to speak around the gag.

Limon smiled. "No need for you to be afraid. Death has chosen you. It has come for you tonight."

Instead of allowing the blood find its own way to drain from the body, or clot up, Limon changed his tactic. He picked up the man's right wrist, carefully slicing the skin open with a scalpel, making the man moan. When he used a tool to carefully lift the ulnar artery and slide the cannula in, the man stiffened up. Tears drained down the sides of his face.

Limon allowed the artery to ooze back under the flesh.

Locating the beat of the man's heart using two fingers he sliced open the jugular vein. The man's blood filled the troughs on both sides of the table.

When Limon switched on the embalming machine, it pumped out the blood, quickly snuffing out the hitch-hiker's life, which was diminishing.

CHAPTER ELEVEN

———————————

Tobias stood across from his destination.

He sucked in a deep breath, blew it out. He checked out the street, not seeing a soul. Cars lined both sides of the street, except for a few in the driveways. Things were quiet, except for a small breeze blowing leaves in the trees. It was a complete three sixty from what he was used to: loud machinery, pleading and begging from the others who complained they could not go on, could not continue working under the hot sun. Ones who came down sick with disease or had physical problems or were hauled away and stuffed into the Building, a place of torture and death.

If sleep ever deprived him of nightmares, each day in his future world surely delivered them.

As the memories returned, once more in remembrance of the end of humanity on Earth, the end of his home before the attack, they quickly clawed their way back to the surface...

Memoirs: Part 2

Tobias drove the backroads. The only way he knew of an escape.

The Honda rolled to a stop. A deep crater lay in the road, no doubt from a laser blast. Inside the hole a car billowed smoke and flame.

Something smelled horrible.

Katie whined. Max barked.

"I know guys, we'll find a good road to drive on to find shelter," Tobias tried to assure them, as well as himself.

Thunder cracked across the sky. In the distance, an explosion rumbled the ground.

Tobias turned the car around and found a street into a suburb. A pile of cars sat burning, blocking one street. Another bore more craters in the road. Even a few empty lots where houses originally sat.

Tobias whipped into an alley.

Debris was scattered everywhere. Overturned trash cans rolled back and forth, their contents emptied, covering the pavement. A great big green plastic job rolled in front of the Honda and Tobias swerved to miss, but the right front tire caught it.

"Damnit!" Tobais cursed.

They emerged and turned onto a street leading them in another direction toward another road. Hopefully a way of escape.

The Honda passed more houses and more vehicles, all ablaze. A horrible smell lingered in the air. The same one leaking from that hole in the road.

Tobias now realized what it had been, observing a pile of burning carcasses.

The stench stole his breath.

Tobias coughed, fighting back a puke, and returned to the back roads. Ahead, the road curved. He drove the Honda fast around a curve and the back end slid. He had to adjust his steering,

Max barked.

"Hush, Max," Tobias said. "We're okay."

Katie whined. "That goes for you, too, big girl," he added.

The road declined and the car carried them into a pocket, then around another small curve, and over another hill.

Max barked again. Before Tobias could scold him again, a large shadow fell over the car.

"Shit!" Tobias spat.

A green blast fell from the sky and blasted the earth away and the vibration rumbled behind the Honda as it hit the bottom of a hill and climbed another. Another blast ripped beside the passenger side window causing the small car to jerk to the right.

Tobias fought the wheel to control the car. He prevented a crash into a ditch.

Another hill appeared, this one very big.

Tobias mashed the accelerator, shoving the car faster, revving the small engine and it climbed. At the top the alien ship roared over and unleashed a blast, slamming the hood causing the small car to flip end over end, making it airborne.

Max and Katie bounced off the roof and seats

Tobias's seatbelt squeezed, shoving air from his lungs.

The pavement reached through the windshield.

Tobias screamed.

Max's yelping followed Katie's.

The Honda slammed into the soft ground off the road upside down, crunching the ceiling. The windshield shattered into billions of little pieces, slicing Tobias's face, arms, and hands. Katie's body was sucked out of the passenger window, down a hill into a patch of trees. Max's thick frame hit Tobias, almost knocking him unconscious, then hit the inside of the car.

Something snap inside the canine's body.

The dog howled.

With the momentum of the impact the Honda followed Katie's tumble and rolled down the hill.

Max hit the ceiling, the front passenger seat, then the ceiling again, howling.

Tobias heard more bones snap inside the canine's body.

Max was jerked into the backseat, ending his howling after a long, drawn out moan until it snapped off.

The Honda crashed through trees and rolled nearly forever until a large oak became a concrete stop, crunching the passenger side.

Tobias could smell gas and radiator fluid. Smoke billowed from the hood. Tobias noticed he had bent the wheel with his tight grip. He tried to unsnap the seatbelt.

It wouldn't release.

Flames ignited in the smoke.

Another try to release the belt failed.

Thunder cracked across the skies.

Tobias wondered if the ship was making a return visit, making sure it had murdered everyone in the car.

Frantic, he fought with the belt. No release from its hold.

Then...

He remembered his pocket knife. He reached in his front pocket, took it out.

It took forever to cut through, but it finally fell away. Damn did his chest ache. He peeled himself from the seat and out the driver's window.

He crawled on all fours away from the car to a tree.

He tried to stand and his knees buckled. His body felt one big bruise. His back throbbed.

Had he broken part of his spine? he wondered. No. That couldn't be. Wouldn't have been able to move.

He glanced at the car. Poor Max. God only knew where poor Katie ended up.

In the distance, thunder cracked.

Were they finished with him? Were they flying away? ....whupwhupwhupwhup!

Flames grew larger under the hood of the Honda.

Tobias couldn't pull himself up the hill, toward the

road. On both sides of the road lay wooded areas. Above, something was coming.

Whupwhupwhupwhup...

The closer it drew, the more terror sunk in. He rose, his legs finally working, and he staggered, but fell back down.

Damnit.... need to get moving. He'd be a sitting duck if didn't...

In less than a half hour Tobias had lost his home and his dog in one short burst. Maybe it was time to die, he thought. Maybe it was time for god to take him. Time to allow the dirt to shower over him.

As he crawled across the road, his face and hands still bleeding, the sound grew louder, closing distance.

Tobias looked over his shoulder.

Over the tree tops a military helicopter appeared and circled before landing in the middle of the road, almost a hundred feet away. Three soldiers ran toward him. One asked if he could walk.

I...don't think so, he replied.

They carried him to the helicopter. Someone worked on him. There was a small sting in the bend of his arm. The same someone held an IV bag. The same someone assured he would be okay now. They were taking him to

—he blacked out.

And woke up in a place called the Shelter, a place where survivors of Earth stayed. Days became a few months before the invaders located it and murdered many, including the president of the United States.

Tobias' life upended. He worked under a hot sun for an alien race wishing to develop a new world.

Thus, began the slow the slow extinction of the human species.

Tobias used a small packet of tools, popped the lock to the door, and walked inside.

CHAPTER TWELVE

L imon placed the embalmed body of the hitchhiker in one of the three caskets. He closed the door, and no sooner placed his foot on the first step to go upstairs when he heard footsteps above.

Limon could have sworn he had locked the front and back doors. No one should be here.

At the long counter where the embalming machine sat, he pulled out a drawer. His hand reached in, grabbed what he needed and climbed the stairs. He opened the basement door a crack, enough to peek through. He didn't see anyone and swung the door wider, while the hinges let out a low whine.

A shadow passed in the kitchen.

Limon walked into the room where Madelyn lay locked inside of her casket and stepped toward the kitchen, squeezing the handle of his knife.

The faucet ran.

CHAPTER THIRTEEN

Tobias stepped inside. The refrigerator's compressor hummed. Clean dishes sat in a drainer. Somewhere, a clock ticked. The kitchen was a throwback from the sixties, never updated. Bright-colored base units with antiqued cherry cabinets and the workstation a smaller-size countertop.

Tobias stopped.

He heard a noise in the other room.

CHAPTER FOURTEEN

"Here kind of late, aren't you?" Limon stood on the threshold into the kitchen. Mark stumbled back, almost dropping a glass of water. "Damn. You scared me!"

Limon slid the blade into his back pocket. "Did I? Sorry."

"Yeah, man." he chuckled. "I had to come back. Forgot my book." He tapped a finger on the book on the counter, *The Principles and Practice of Embalming*.

"Oh…Well, can't very well go to school without your book, can you?" Limon grinned.

"Nope, Mr. Fisher will kill me."

"Fisher is a decent guy. He'd probably give you some shit, then hand you his copy."

"You think he would? The guy doesn't strike me as being a professor who cares about his students. Some of the others have names for him. Like Fisher the Fool; Fisher—"

"The Ripper."

"Yeah, that's it. Know about that name, too?"

"The Ripper taught me how to do this job, Michael. Whether you or the other kids believe that he can, or cannot do the job, he has the experience needed to teach you all. Don't short change the guy."

Mark shook his head, held his hand up, in defense. "Oh, don't worry, that's not what we think—least, I know *I* don't think that. On the first day of school, I could tell right off he was a good teacher."

"Good. Listen to the guy because he has seen a lot of weird shit. Fisher used to work here, with me. Or, better, I used to work with him. I don't know if you have heard this tale or not.… but…about ten years ago there was a bus load of kids on the way to school who were creamed by a dump truck doing sixty miles an hour."

Mark frowned. "I think my dad told me that story. Those kids died, right?"

"Yes. Even the bus driver. The guy driving the dump truck passed out, rolled across the grassy median, hit the bus head-on."

"Wow! I remember Dad saying that, now."

"If the guy had hit the ditch, only a hundred or so yards ahead, his truck would have missed the bus, flipped over, crushing him, taking out one life instead of ten."

"Right."

"The accident was the worst thing that this area had ever seen."

"No one survived?"

"Nope. Everyone inside the bus burned to death."

"Did the dump truck driver live?"

"No. He died on impact."

"That's awful…"

"We had a mess on our hands, Michael, collecting pieces of kids, trying to find out who was who."

"Man, that's terrible." Michael shook his head again. "Well," He sat his empty glass on the sink. "I guess I better get going. See you tomorrow, Limon."

"I'll be here."

He turned to leave, then: "What time do I need to be here tomorrow?"

"Come on in at seven, if you would, so we can load the flowers and wait on the relatives. I think the Mrs. Madelyn Grey's children are going to be the pallbearers."

"Okay. Later," Mark gave a wave and walked over to the front door.

Limon strode behind him.

Mark stopped. "Crap! I left something downstairs earlier."

"What did you leave?"

"My watch." He tapped his wrist. I'll be right back."

Before Limon could catch him, telling him he'd be glad to go down and grab the watch, Mark hurried into the basement.

CHAPTER FIFTEEN

Tobias heard the sound again.

Light from a street lamp spilled through open curtains, highlighting half the living room. His eyes strained to make out the outline of a tall lamp sat by the front door. A recliner sat below it. A couch sat along the far wall and two bookcases stuffed with books filled the void on each side.

Tobias stepped toward one of the bookcases, cracked his shin on the coffee table, grumbled.

Some of the books were classics like *To Kill a Mockingbird* and *Moby Dick*. Others were about embalming and other resources of the craft. He touched the spine of one novel, attempted to pull it free, froze.

The sound returned, the front doorknob jiggled.

CHAPTER SIXTEEN

The kidnapper had trouble picking the lock, finally opening it.

He shut the door behind him. Once Limon returned home, he would need to talk to him. He needed to inform him of the rebellion sending someone to kill him. He took a few more steps before a pain exploded in the back of his head, sending him crashing the floor.

Tobias kicked him in the gut.

The kidnapper grabbed hold of his attacker's leg, jerked back.

Tobias slammed the floor. The vibration knocked a TV off the coffee table. The kidnapper grabbed Tobias by the neck, used his other hand punched him in the face.

Stars burst in Tobias' vision.

Another punch cracked a tooth and another broke his nose.

Tobias used his legs to pull the attacker backward by wrapping them around his head. Twisting, he slid away.

"Stay where you are so I can kill you, Tobias." The attacker rose, the same weapon used to kill the family in his grip.

How'd he know my name? Tobias scrambled into the kitchen.

CHAPTER SEVENTEEN

Mark didn't know what to say. Or feel. Except shock. Why would the caskets be in this back room? Why would there be a corpse in one?

All he needed was his watch. Not this. He questioned the pile of clothes on the floor, then curiosity ended inside this room. What the hell was Limon doing? Keeping a secret stash of the dead? Who the heck *was* this guy he saw?

"Mark."

The boy jumped.

Limon stood in the doorway. "What are you doing in here, Mark?"

"I-I was just trying to find my watch."

"Your watch isn't in here. It's on the counter behind me, close to our embalming table."

"R-Right."

Fear crawled under Mark's flesh. Could he get

around Limon? Would he be able to make a run for it?

"Well…um…I guess I should probably get my watch, huh?"

"Sounds like a great idea, Mark."

Limon stepped to the side. "Go ahead, grab it."

Mark wasn't sure whether to move or not. He glanced at the corpse again.

"I'm giving you a chance to walk out of here, Mark. If you can forget what you see in here, it's good."

Mark blinked.

"The deal is for you to not ask me anything. Grab your watch and walk upstairs."

The funeral director knew Mark desperately searched for an explanation about the dead hitchhiker. The boy wanted to know why there were three caskets by themselves in an old, musty room that had not been used for years. Would he be trusted to walk out of here and not say anything? Sure, anything is possible.

Mark hadn't moved any further.

"Mark, go ahead and grab your watch."

Mark stepped forward.

"But no questions."

Mark nodded and slipped by Limon, grabbed his watch.

"Tomorrow at seven, Mark. don't be late." The door to the room shut.

"Sure. I'll…. see you then, huh?"

Limon nodded.

Halfway up the stairs Limon said, "Stop."

Mark obeyed.

"Do you wish to question me about the hidden room?"

Mark wished to—really wanted to—but said, "Nope. I'm good. I'll see ya tomorr—"

"Aren't you even slightly curious?" Limon stepped forward.

"Nope. Not anymore. I'm not going to ask you any questions. That's part of the deal, right?"

"Yes, it is—or was. To be fair, since you're my employee you could be entitled to ask me a question. Why not? We've had a good relationship. Correct?"

"Yeah." Mark snatched a glance at the top step, at the door. The one that would allow him to step through. The one that'd allow him to get away from his boss. Could he make a run for it? Call the police? "Nope, I'm not curious anymore. I'm not going to ask you any questions. I consider it none of my business."

"Well, Mark, I gave it some thought. I was wrong. Maybe I should answer your questions. I should fill you in what exactly I am doing down here."

Limon took another step forward.

CHAPTER EIGHTEEN

The kidnapper stepped into the kitchen. "You humans won't win. We know the Rebellions' whereabouts." He flicked on the overhead light.

And it wasn't who Tobias was after.

"You aren't Limon."

"No, my Rebellion friend, I am not. Thought you'd sneak up on our prize pupil and take him out, did you? We knew one of you humans were going to make a trip in the past to stop Limon. You're too late. There is no way you will stop his killings. They are in motion, helping the future to be under our control."

"We were careful not showing you freaks we had a time machine."

"I think the right word is careless, Tobias. You can thank your buddy Thatch. It took some persuading, but he finally came around. Thatch spilled everything about the machine. He even gave us a bonus: where the Rebellion hideout was. Now you have nowhere to return to, Tobias. Your life ends tonight. You will be part of the past; never a part of the future.

"Don't move, this is only going to hurt once."

The kidnapper reached for Tobias. Shifting left, Tobias kicked his attacker's legs out from under him and he brought his elbow down on the bridge of the attacker's nose.

Tobias wrenched the knife away from his opponent and stuck it in the kidnapper's chest. The kidnapper didn't cry out. He didn't feel pain. He wore someone's else's flesh, skin which took the wounds.

Tobias stabbed his attacker again. A hand grabbed his throat and jerked him to the side, letting him go, making slide across the linoleum and crash into the stove.

The kidnapper grabbed the knife, working on his opponent.

CHAPTER NINETEEN

Mark decided he didn't wish to ask Limon a question. He didn't wish to hear what Limon had been up to. So, he made a run for it, launching himself up the stairs. He reached for the doorknob and when his fingertips brushed it Limon had grabbed hold and yanked him backward.

Mark tumbled and the back of his head smacked the hard floor.

"You could have asked a question, buddy. I would have allowed it. No kidding. But dashing away, well, I just cannot have that."

Mark's head spun. The back of his head throbbed.

"You see, Mark, death is the business to be in. What choice do people have at the end of their roads? What choice do they have when they are sick and diseased? What choice do they have when the cancer is eating them from inside? Death always reigns true. Its talent is remarkable. That is why I adore Death. I worship Death.

Death takes no prisoners. I take no prisoners, especially when I have the joy of ending their life in this very room.

"On that," he pointed to the embalming table, "you can watch one gasp their very last breath, their very last bit of oxygen God has allowed to drain into their lungs on the day of their birth. It is such an extraordinary thing, Death."

A pain shot down Mark's leg when he tried to move.

"Mark," Limon bent down close to him, "I am not what I seem to be. Not exactly what I portray to be."

"You're crazy!"

"Not exactly. Let me see if I can come up with a better one…" Limon pressed his hands together as if praying. "One that would explain things…*better*." Limon touched his lips with the tips of his fingers and glanced at the ceiling. "I know! Check this out, kid. You'll love it."

The skin on Limon's face withered; shed from its bone. His clothes fell away, revealing his nakedness, though only for a second, if not more, until the skin yellowed and streaked green, becoming a hairless creature, whose sex was unknown. Its neck stretched and the eyeless skull become oblong. Its arms grew and the hands claws.

The monstrosity opened a palm, revealed a triple set of yellow eyes.

A long slice ripped open along its stomach.

"Not to worry, kid," it lips gurgled around a drain of thick black saliva, "Limon is still under here." The skin shifted above the mouth and the outline of Limon's face appeared, then sunk back in. "I am called Zifir, Mark. I traveled from the future and possessed this body not long ago. My species will arrive here in your future, decades from now and take over this planet.

"I see you do not have the right colors of aura to be attached to, controlled," The flesh wrinkled as the stomach frowned. "Very sad. I would spare you and send another one of my species to invade your flesh, but you do not have the aura. Not your lucky day, kiddo."

Zifir grabbed Mark around the throat and squeezed.

Mark tried to pry the claws from his throat.

Zifir gurgled as Mark slipped into darkness.

CHAPTER TWENTY

The pain switched from intense to a growing numbness.

The blade slide in, the blade slid out.

Tobias choked as blood filled his throat. Dying on the kitchen floor, the world darkened.

A second later the flash of a bright light blinded the kidnapper.

CHAPTER TWENTY-ONE

M orphed back in the human form of Limon, Zifir found his front door unlocked and used caution before stepping a foot inside.

Two bodies lay on the kitchen floor.

"Don't move," a voice spoke behind him.

"What do you want? Who the hell are those two on my floor?"

"One is a good friend of mine. The other was a victim your one of your species kidnapped."

"Species? What the hells are you talking about?"

A light green blast skinned the body of flesh and clothes, revealing an orb, once alive, now a pitch black, dead thing. "Don't be naive, Limon." A dark-haired man in a black tight-fitting spandex suit faced him. He was armed with a pistol. "I know what you really are, Limon." The dead thing fell apart, scattering into tiny pieces. "I killed your friend here after he killed mine. If I was only a second sooner, if the old Body Launcher, hadn't sputtered when Thatch hit the button, my friend would still be alive.

"Yours, though, would still be very dead."

"I've no idea what you're talking about. I'm not even sure why you are in my home. What do you want? Money?"

Ignoring the question, he replied "My friend there was sent to kill you. I was sent here to make sure the job was done."

"Kill me? Why? I've done nothing."

"Right. Keep telling yourself that and maybe the lie will stick. Doubt it, though. Hiding behind the truth won't help your situation. Never does." He gestured with his gun. "We're taking a ride. I'll use a vacuum cleaner on your friend, but mine, I need to bury and you're gonna help me."

"Why should I?"

The dark-haired man pointed the gun at Limon's forehead. "Your life will depend on it."

"Look, whoever you are, you're making a mistake."

"No, I'm not. I have my target. Get moving." He waved the gun.

Three steps toward the door and a bright light flashed, blinding them both. The light oozed away and a young boy stood there.

"Where'd you come from?" the dark-headed man asked.

The boy blinked. Then blinked once more before moving his lips. "I'm...not quite sure." For quite a while

—Days? Months? A year? —he had been part of dark tales, some quite horrifying. And now they were slowly sliding away, forgotten bits and pieces of memories.

"Are you from my world, kid?"

"*Where's* your world?"

The guy explained it, including the fact he was a time traveler.

"Um. Nope. I'm not from there."

"Where did you come from then?"

The boy's explanation had the time traveler scratching his head, especially what had happened to him by some weird little guy calling himself Dittle Tek, an evil twin who looked closely like a friend from the kid's time period. And the odd set of words, the Multi-Colored Positronic Brain Waves.

"So, this guy stuck you in stories?" the dark-haired man asked.

"Yep," Selwyn responded. "Like I'm part of a tale inside a book or something. Freaky odd."

"Freaky odd; good way to put it."

"So," Limon drew in a breath, let it out, stuck a finger on his lips, "you aren't from the future? But," he looked at the time traveler, "you are." He smiled. "Interesting."

"You don't know the half of what interesting can be, Limon. I'm not through with you yet."

"Hey, I'm just an observer here. I'm innocent. Trust me, kid." He winked.

"Don't listen to him," the dark-haired man said.

"This man is a killer and I'm here to end his body count."

"Don't listen to him, kid. He broke into my home. He wants to rob me, too."

Selwyn also noticed something else.

"Um…and who is on the floor?"

"A good friend of mine who got killed."

"Who did it?'

"One of his kind. See that debris on the floor? It used to be an alien species."

"Oh. Wow."

"This guy is trying to frame me with murders," Limon said.

"Shut up, Limon," the dark-haired man instructed.

"I'm one of the good guys. He's the imposter!" Limon pointed a finger. "We need to call 911. Kid, do me a favor and grab my cellphone out of my inside pocket."

"What if he shoots me?"

"He's not *that* stupid."

"I wouldn't advise you doing that," the dark-haired man said. "I'm telling you the truth about this guy. Please, keep your distance."

"Don't listen to him." Limon said, taking a step. "Look at this scene. Look what's going on. He's pointing a gun at *me*. You can even check to see if I'm armed if you wish. That'd prove I'm not the bad guy. I mean, c'mon, I'm the good guy here."

The dark-haired man glanced at Selwyn, opened his mouth to prove once again Limon was indeed the bad guy here, and didn't need to. Limon revealed the truth. He grabbed Selwyn.

"Hey! Let me go!"

"You're not going anywhere, kid," placing a head-lock on Selwyn. "You're my ticket outta here."

"Let the kid go, Limon. He is no concern to you."

"Oh, but he is. He's an insurance policy. If you want to see him alive, you best drop your gun. Now."

The gun did not waver.

Limon used his other arm and pinched Selwyn's head, making him gag. "I'll end his life right now.

The dark-haired man scowled. "Limon. This is between me and you. Got it? Let him go."

"You wish to chance this mortal's life, eh? I'll kill him right here. Right now."

Selwyn's face reddened. He gagged.

"Drop the gun." Limon warned.

The gun clattered to the floor.

Limon switched positions by letting go of Selwyn's but grabbing his wrist. "Pick up the gun, kid. Give it to me."

Selwyn felt a squeeze.

"Or I will break your wrist."

Selwyn gave the guy a mean look.

Limon returned one. "Wanna try me, kid?"

Selwyn's wrist hurt.

"Get your ass over there and pick up the gun *now*!"

Selwyn obeyed, wondering if his hand would fall off.

"After I kill you," Limon raised the gun at the time

traveler and jerked Selwyn to the side, letting go of his wrist, "I'm gonna use your device to return to the future and start picking off the Rebellion one by one. They won't know what hit them. I will find out your secret location. I will be awarded by my species. I may become the king." Limon laughed. "Say goodbye to this guy, kid. He's history."

Selwyn couldn't let this happen. He tackled him, as best as he could, being half the man's size.

Limon managed to pull the trigger, but the bullet crashed through the front window.

The dark-haired man stomped on Limon's hand, felt bones break, and grabbed the gun.

"Sorry about that. Should have listened to you."

"No worries, kid. I'm just glad you are okay." He stuck out a hand. "I'm Fremont."

"I'm Selwyn."

They shook hands.

"What you just did here has saved a lot of people. Consider yourself a hero, Selwyn."

Selwyn felt good and beamed.

"You don't need to watch what I'm gonna do to this guy. Selwyn. We need to part ways here. I'm gonna take care of Limon and teleport back home."

"Oh, okay," he replied. "So…you're from the future?"

"Yup. Bad times there, Selwyn. Very bad times. I'll spare you the terrors. Sounds like what you're dealing with, that guy you mentioned, is enough. Especially for a child."

"Okay."

"Catch you later, Selwyn. Thanks again." Fremont grinned. "Get outta here. Good luck in your travels, kid."

"See ya." Selwyn stepped through the front door and never saw Fremont or Limon again. But heard the gunshot.

~

"Is it done, Freemont?"

"Yeah. Couldn't save Tobias, though. One of those creatures murdered him before I arrived."

"His death is on me, man. I couldn't get the machine to launch you quick enough."

"Tobias was a good guy."

"That, he was."

"I'm returning, man. Be there in," he checked his watch, "Oh six hundred and fifteen, your time, Thatch."

"Copy on that. See you when you get here. Miller said he has another job for you. Some killer who loves collecting hands from his victims."

"Huh. Interesting hobby."

"Tell me about it."

"See you when I see you, Thatch."

"Copy, Freemont."

Fremont swiped the screen on the Samsung, cutting the transmission and waited for the bright light to materialize, snatching him into the future.

SELWYN, CONCLUSION

The second Selwyn stepped over the threshold the Hula Hoop Obitor clattered to Selwyn's feet. A stream of water slipped down his back.

Dittle Tek wasn't alone. Two skinless, humanoid-shaped creatures accompanied him. Three feet above each of their heads a baseball-size chrome sphere hovered, expelling a buzz with every turn, similar to an inhabited bee hive.

The sensation crawl down Selwyn's spine.

The humanoid creatures' yellow cyclopean eyes blinked above shaved off noses. Glancing at Selwyn slices opened and pulled back into grins, revealing an army of serrated knives. Their giggles expelled saliva from their lips and when the spheres gyrated, flashing multiple colors, small cuts in their wet flesh opened and bled.

If one tried deciphering the sex of these two bodies,

the intestines hung over the crotch hiding the option.

"So very nice to see you again, Selwyn." Dittle Tek beamed. "How was your adventure? Enticing? Thrilling? Fun? I do hope the answer is 'Yes.'" He winked and his large smiled spread across half his face showing bleach-white teeth.

Selwyn didn't respond, his attention elsewhere.

"Oh, are you afraid of these two?" —he gestured with a wave of his hand— "They are nothing to be worried with. Harmless, less they don't like someone."

Their spheres stopped moving.

"It appears they enjoy your company, though; especially smiling like that. Allow me to share with you their names so you can be more acquainted: this is Trials; and this Tribulation. A pair of twins who love inflicting self pain and suffering. They are from the same dimension I retrieved the Hula Hoop. Kinda odd how we became friends, eh?"

He glanced at Trials.

Trials' smile did not widen or drop.

"They are from a post-apocalyptic developed by four creatures, each riding inside their own transparent sphere. Quite an interesting place.

"I stumbled upon these two by accident, stepping into a small ripple in the Waves. They were being held against their will by an awful fella. One thing led to another, and I was able to help these two out. They wanted to hang out with me, so, here we are. One big happy family of three. You will make four, my boy."

The duo continued to grin.

The spheres gyrated again and buzzed. More small cuts appeared.

"Anyways, these two can take more pain and more suffering than anyone or *anything* in who live and breathe in the world of the Multi-Colored Brain Waves. Or, probably, any type of world known.

"I put my oath on it. Wonderful beings these two are, don't you think?"

The creatures blinked; grinned with a mouthful of blood instead of saliva.

Oddly, their spheres stopped, gyrated backward, developing scabs over their inflictions.

"Any individual who I might think could become an asset to my family I collect." Dittle Tek frowned. "I wonder how you will fair for a long life with me and the others? Could you become useful? Could we become close friends? We have become good friends, have we not?"

Selwyn did not reply.

"Aw, c'mon! We could eventually be *best friends*. You'd enjoy it, my boy. I think you and I can make something work. Trials and Tribulation needs someone to talk to, anyway. See how bored they can be?"

The sphere shifted a fourth time, tearing open the scabs.

Playtime with those things? Selwyn thought. Hell no! "Let me go, Dittle Tek. I want to go home."

"Child, you do not need to return to that awful world. You said you hated being there. You said it your-self: the town was dull. You are tired of that bully picking on you. Nothing ever happened in your town. A population of a whopping two thousand—including the livestock!" He burst out laughing. "I'm only helping your life become better. And with those two, I couldn't imagine your life ever being dull. Selwyn, my boy, I do believe another adventure awaits you. Follow me," curling a finger Dittle Tek took three steps.

Selwyn did not move.

"Move, or I will have my friends suck the flesh off your fingers, one by one."

Trials licked his lips.

Tribulation burped.

And grinned.

Selwyn moved.

"Good boy." Smile. "Come, allow us to accompany you over to the carousel. Time's a waistin'. You're about to receive another nightmare—I mean *fun adventure*—which is just *oozing* for your welcome. You have a variety of selections, kiddo, each are new developments. My upgrades. Go sit on a character of your choice, take off. Each adventure will be brand new. Ain't nothing you've ever seen before. Nothing you've ever read in those books you like or watched on film." He bent sideways, stuck his hand against his mouth, spoke out the side of his mouth, whispered: "If I was you, I'd choose one of those gnomes there in between the two clowns, the one on a motor bike with a side car. You could slip inside that puppy and relax during your ride."

Dittle Tek beamed.

Selwyn did not wish to sit on anything on the carousel. Much less inside that car attached to the motor bike.

The figures on the carousel turned their heads, watched him.

The horse neighed.

The three-horned unicorn neighed and Selwyn coulda sworn he heard it giggle.

Ribbons of steam curled from the dragon's nose as it grunted.

The lycanthrope growled and showed its teeth.

The clowns grinned, stuck out their tongues.

The gnomes winked.

"Choose, Selwyn, or the choice will be made for you," Dittle Tek instructed.

Selwyn stepped onto the carousel, climbed on, and tasted salt water.

ABOUT THE AUTHOR

Brick Marlin lives in Southern Indiana with his lovely wife and their two shelties, Daphne and Sir Ronnie. Not only is his passion writing bizarre tales, he's also an avid blues harmonica player in a local blues band, an avid trail runner, and an avid biker.